THE SCORPION KILLERS

**Center Point
Large Print**

**This Large Print Book carries the
Seal of Approval of N.A.V.H.**

THE SCORPION KILLERS

RAY HOGAN

CENTER POINT PUBLISHING
THORNDIKE, MAINE

Library of Congress Cataloging-in-Publication Data

Hogan, Ray, 1908-
  The scorpion killers / Ray Hogan.
     p. cm.
  Originally published: New York : Signet, 1974.
  ISBN 978-1-60285-607-3 (library binding : alk. paper)
  1. Large type books. I. Title.

PS3558.O3473S36 2009
813'.54--dc22

2009024424

1

Moody, Starbuck sat alone at his table in El Paso's Longhorn Saloon and absently twirled an empty whiskey glass between a thumb and forefinger. It was just past midmorning in the small border town and there were no more than half a dozen other patrons in the place.

He had found no trace of his brother, not on the Mexican side of the line or in the Texas settlement either; inquiries made in adjacent areas had also proved fruitless—and there had been no word of him for months. Seemingly, Ben had vanished from the face of the earth.

Always before during the long years he had been conducting a patient search for the brother who now called himself Damon Friend he had been able occasionally to turn up news of him, bits of information that gave hope, and sometimes he had come near to effecting a meeting; but now there was a total absence of such clues.

Wyoming, Kansas, Texas, a dozen or more other states and territories—he had crossed and criss-crossed them all in the quest, pausing only to take a job when funds ran low and then, when able, faithfully resuming the search for Ben, who had left home at the age of sixteen after a quarrel with their father, Hiram.

Hiram had died not long afterward, leaving in

trust for his two sons a fair-sized legacy, but with the provision that it was not to be shared until both presented themselves to the designated trustees. Shawn, seven years his brother's junior, had so far devoted his life to the cause.

But now, with all the endless wandering behind him, Shawn Starbuck was beginning to wonder, to doubt. Was it worth it? Would he not be better off to settle down, to accept one of the many offers of a good job that had been tendered him, and start building a life of his own?

A boy who had been crystallized quickly into a man by the harsh frontier, turned expert by experience along the lonely trails he had ridden, he could choose and become about anything he wished: lawman, bullion guard, hired gun, outrider, wagon-master, trail boss, cowhand, guide—he had done them all, and successfully.

Apparently Shawn's efforts to get in touch with Ben meant nothing to him. It was hard to believe that after so long a time his brother could be unaware of the search he was making, since Shawn had left word in many places to that effect, but with no results. If Ben, still carrying a grudge against Hiram, and evidently extending it to his brother, didn't care, why should he?

His share of the estate, something over fifteen thousand dollars, would be welcome, of course. Receiving it would enable him to do many things he'd dreamed of, permit him to go into the cattle business, in fact, without the slow, tedious building-up that ordinarily went with starting a ranch. Or, if he decided not to follow that line of endeavor, he could simply stash the money away in a bank somewhere, draw on it as he needed cash, while he continued to drift until he found what he did want.

Not having it, however, would be no overwhelming privation. He'd lived this long by his own wits and labor, and while it would be a fine thing to have all that money ready and available anytime he needed it, he'd likely live just as long without it—perhaps even longer.

It occurred to him, as it had before, that Ben could be dead. On previous occasions, though, something had always developed to prove otherwise. Here again there was a difference; he had heard absolutely nothing of him for months—not since he had disappeared in Tucson shortly after leaving his job with a mining company in Wickenburg. That something had happened to him was becoming a more distinct possibility.

Raising his eyes, Shawn let his glance move slowly about the dimly lit saloon. Two cowhands were at the bar, in conversation with the man behind it. The discussion evidently had to do with the pair of steer horns that were mounted on the wall above the back mirror. Doubtlessly they would measure a full seven feet from tip to tip, and served as the source of the establishment's name, the Longhorn Saloon.

Two more men were at a nearby table, laughing and talking with a woman, while at the one immediately next to his a young Mexican, dressed in vaquero garb, also sat alone—and also with problems on his mind.

A kindred soul, Starbuck thought, studying him covertly. He was a lean, cool-looking individual, probably about his own age, with the usual dark skin, hair, and eyes of his race. The clothing he wore—white silk shirt, leather jacket, cord and doeskin saddle breeches, knee-high boots—had been expensive when new, and the mark of a gentleman, but now they showed wear. His peak-crowned hat had a bullet hole in its rolled brim, but the pistol visible on his hip was silver-plated and bone-handled. . . . The son of some *hidalgo* down on his luck, Shawn concluded, and turned back to his own thoughts.

What next? There was no point in crossing the Rio Grande and resuming the search for Ben on Mexican soil. He had ridden from Nogales to Juarez, making all the in-between stops and asking for his brother as best he could with his smattering of Spanish, and learned nothing. Later he'd toured the New Mexico and Texas settlements with no better luck, and ended up finally in El Paso. Now, with a long week in the border town behind him with no word, he was stalled.

It seemed a dead end and it would appear that the wandering star under which he seemed to have

8

been born had finally burned itself out, leaving him with no beckoning light.

He could cut back west, he supposed, head toward California on the possibility that his brother, searching for new fields, had pointed in that direction. So far as he knew, Ben had never been in that area, at least rumor had never placed him there, and he could have taken it in mind to try his luck in the state where it was said gold could still be found. Or he could have gone on to Oregon, or perhaps Washington. Still, it was logical to believe someone would have marked his passage through Arizona, yet no one had. It could be—

"Senor—"

Starbuck looked up as the vaquero moved into the chair opposite him at his table, doing it quickly, smoothly.

"Your pardon," the Mexican murmured, lowering his head. "I would ask a favor."

The man spoke careful English in the precise, stilted way of those educated by tutors.

"Sure—"

"Those men in the doorway—"

Starbuck slid a glance to the front of the saloon. Two Mexicans, dressed in dusty, dark business suits, small-brimmed hats, belted pistols about their waists, had halted just inside the entrance. Both had hard-cornered features and small dark eyes with which they were probing the room.

"I see them. What—"

"They seek me—to kill. If you will permit it, I shall sit here with you. It is possible they will not notice me."

2

Shawn stared at the Mexican, frowned. "Kill you! Why?"

The vaquero shook his head. "It is a long story, senor, one that—" Abruptly his words broke off. Then, "They come."

Starbuck pushed back from the table, giving himself greater freedom of movement. He had no idea what it was all about, other than the brief statement the vaquero had made, but two against one—those were odds that needed changing.

The pair in the doorway separated, crossed the room slowly, took positions on either side of the vaquero. They were older men, and there was an unmistakable ruthlessness to them. The one to Shawn's left brushed back the tail of his coat, obviously to make the heavy pistol hanging at his side more accessible. The other, somewhat younger, with a short pointed beard and brushy moustache, folded his arms over his chest and looked on in cold silence as his partner spoke.

"Arturo Jose Dominguez?" he said, along with several words in Spanish.

The young Mexican shrugged, nodded, replied in

like tongue. Both men drew up in evident satisfaction. The bearded one swung his attention to Starbuck.

"You are not the American who rides with this one and his friends," he said after a few moments' narrow study.

"Maybe I am, maybe not."

"You are not as described to us. . . . You would do well to choose your friends better, senor."

"Doing my own picking's a habit of mine," Shawn drawled. Elsewhere in the saloon there was complete quiet as bartender and customers alike looked on. "What's this all about?"

"It is no affair of yours."

"Making it mine—leastwise until I know what the tally is," Starbuck answered coolly, and allowed his left hand to drop carelessly upon the weapon at his side.

The older Mexican frowned, shook his head. "It is a mistake, senor. This man, Dominguez, who many call by the name of Bravo, is a murderer. He is wanted for such by my government—"

"A lie!" the vaquero snapped. "It is you assassins and those who hire you that want my death."

"Those who hire us are of the government."

"Another lie," Bravo declared. "They are politicians of small consequence—worms who gnaw away at the foundation of our true government in hopes of furthering their own ambition and greed!"

"Words without meaning!" the bearded Mexican shouted, and continued in a string of rapid Spanish.

Shawn saw Dominguez tense, guessed there had been some sort of threat or command in the words. . . . He could be getting himself involved in something that was none of his business, Shawn realized—Mexican government affairs possibly best left alone by an outsider, especially an American, who, officials below the border were continually complaining, were guilty of meddling all too often. . . . Still, after hearing Bravo's words, there seemed to be some doubt existing as to the authority of the two men, and for the vaquero's sake he wanted that cleared up for his own satisfaction.

"Name's Starbuck," he said, bringing proceedings to an immediate halt. "Like to know who you two are."

The younger man, now pulling back the front of his coat to display the weapon he was wearing well forward on his belly, stiffened angrily. "I am Onofre Pacheco, an agent of the Mexican government."

"I am Cruz Sandoval," the older one added, dropping his arms to his sides. "Also, I am an agent. . . . You will do well not to interfere."

"Agents, perhaps, but first assassins," Bravo muttered.

"They work for your government or not?"

12

"Not for the *Presidente*, but for certain ones of the government who would—"

"*Vamos!*" Pacheco cut in harshly, and reached for Bravo's shoulder.

The vaquero came to his feet in a sudden lunge. Driving his elbow back into the belly of Sandoval, he snatched up his chair, swung it at Pacheco's head. The Mexican jerked aside, endeavored to duck, failed. The piece of furniture smashed into his shoulder, splintered into a dozen parts.

Instantly Bravo whirled, rushed by the gasping Sandoval, and lunged for the saloon's nearby side door. The two men at the counter, as well as the pair with the girl, were watching intently. The bartender, who had hurried to the front entrance, was yelling to someone in the street, evidently summoning a lawman.

Shawn threw a glance at Pacheco. The agent, stunned by the blow he had received, was standing spraddle-legged, head slung forward, hands hanging at his sides. Sandoval, however, only briefly disabled, had recovered and was drawing his pistol.

Starbuck reacted automatically. Grabbing the edge of the table, he flipped it into the man. The impact knocked Sandoval's weapon from his hand, and as he bent to recover it, Shawn spun, legged it for the door through which Bravo had disappeared. He had made himself a part of the affair, whatever its truth, and accordingly it would be foolish to remain there now and accept the consequences.

Men were pouring into the saloon from the street, one of them wearing a star. A tight grin pulled at Starbuck's mouth. He now had the local lawman down on him, as well as the two Mexican agents.

Gaining the exit, he bolted through it just as Sandoval, weapon recovered, snapped a shot at him. The bullet thudded harmlessly into the adobe wall of the saloon a foot above his head. Unhesitating as he broke into the open, he veered toward his horse standing at a hitchrack a dozen strides to his right.

Jerking the reins free, Starbuck vaulted onto the saddle of the sorrel gelding, wheeled away. He caught sight of Bravo, mounted and with two other vaqueros, a hundred yards down a narrow side street just as Sandoval and Pacheco, with a half dozen followers, came through the doorway into the alley.

Immediately, Bravo and the pair with him opened up at the agents. The hail of bullets slammed into the wall of the building around the door, checked the pursuers, sent them scrambling back to safety inside the saloon. Voices were shouting in the street now, and a pall of dust, exploded from the mud-brick wall of the building where the bullets had dug in, was floating lazily in the hot air.

Shawn paused. His chances for escape—on into

14

the town, where he could lose himself in the alleys and streets, or by joining Bravo and his two friends, all beckoning to him—were about even.

Abruptly he brought the sorrel about, spurred toward the vaqueros; whatever he'd gotten himself into, he wanted to know more about; later, if he didn't like the game, he'd pull out.

Gunshots began to hammer as he raced past the side doorway of the saloon, and bullets dug into the powder-dry soil around him, smashing into the ancient walls beyond, but he reached the waiting men untouched. And then, together, they turned and rode hard for the river where densely growing trees and thick underbrush offered protective cover.

3

They rushed on for a good two miles, taking a due north course. Coming to a long, rocky slope, they pounded up onto it, abruptly cut left for the river. Shawn understood immediately; a posse following would lose their tracks on the flinty hillside, would be unsure if they had continued on up the valley or not.

Reaching the first of the huge, spreading cotton-woods, they doubled back until they were again within only a short distance of the settlement, and there, in a well-hidden coulee, drew to a halt and dismounted.

Starbuck, tying the sorrel to a sapling, brushed away the sweat collected on his forehead, glanced about. The vaqueros apparently had been using the place as their camp for some time, judging from the horse droppings and other litter. Turning, he walked back into the center of the small clearing.

Bravo Dominguez, taller and more muscular than he had appeared in the Longhorn, and his two friends were watching him intently. One, a large thick-shouldered man with a brushy, down-curving moustache beneath which broad white teeth gleamed, showed frank hostility. Like Bravo, he also wore a silvered pistol on his hip, while from the opposite side of his belt hung a long, thin-bladed knife.

"My friend, Starbuck," Bravo said, by way of beginning the introductions, and then bucked his head at the big man. "This is Carlos Ortega."

Ortega nodded coolly and Shawn, taking his cue from the man's reserved greeting, did likewise.

"Francisco Gomez," Dominguez finished, laying his hand on the shoulder of the other vaquero. Both Mexicans were dressed very much like Bravo.

Gomez was probably the oldest of the three, a still-faced, small-eyed man of average build. He, too, was armed with pistol and knife. Stolid expression unchanging, he stepped forward, offered his hand.

"*Mucho gusto*," he murmured in soft-edged Spanish.

16

Starbuck took the vaquero's strong clasp into his own, pumped briefly in the manner of the Mexican people. "Pleased to meet you, too," he replied, and shifted his attention to Bravo. "Not sure what kind of a game I've cut myself into. Like to know what it's all about."

Dominguez smiled tautly. "It is not a game, my friend, unless you would call survival a game."

"Sort of gathered that," Shawn said dryly. "What Sandoval and Pacheco said—is it true?"

"*Asesinos!*" Ortega hissed, and spat into the brush. Abruptly he wheeled and strode off toward the horses.

Bravo watched him for a moment, shrugged. "He has a very great hate, this Carlos, but so do we all. It is our life and the hour will come when it will be our death."

"You kill somebody in the Mexican government?"

Dominguez dropped to his haunches, reached into a pocket for cigarette makings. Gomez turned away, joined Ortega, and both then strolled off into the trees in the direction of the road, likely to keep watch. Bravo offered the pouch of tobacco and fold of papers to Shawn, and when they were refused, pointed to a nearby log.

"It is a story of much length. If you will sit—"

Starbuck backed to the fallen tree. Settling himself, he watched Bravo expertly twirl himself a thin, brown cigarette, fire a match with a thumb-

17

nail, hold the small flame to the tip of the cylinder, and inhale deeply. Somewhere in the grove a dove called mournfully.

Dominguez listened to the sound for a moment, then said, "Sandoval and Pacheco, they seek us for the killing of General Andres Jaramillo—El Escorpion he was named by the people—a man as cruel and as ugly as the thing for which he was called."

"A general? No wonder they—"

"Such means little in my country. There are many, even hundreds of generals, only a few of them deserve the rank. All, of course, claim loyalty to the *Presidente*, but most, like the Scorpion, seek only wealth and power for themselves.

"We—Carlos, Francisco, myself, and another of us who is now dead, Felipe Vasquez—once lived with our families in the Joaquin Valley near a village called Escobar. Our fathers had great haciendas—ranches, you would say—with many cattle and sheep and good farming. Such had been owned by their fathers, and their fathers before them.

"All was good. Our families prospered and were happy, as were the peons, and then came the French, and all was taken from us—confiscated. We were reduced to poverty, forced into hiding. It was so for years until again there was revolution and the government became that of Benito Juarez and those who followed him. The French were driven out and men of our own people became our leaders, but many were false and secretly hoped to replace Juarez themselves or with someone they could control—and so the turbulence continued.

"In the beginning of Juarez the property of my father and that of my *compadres'* fathers was restored and we at once began the rebuilding. But with the death of Juarez and the changes that began to occur, we one day found ourselves again the victims of oppression—this time by El Escorpion who, in the name of the state, occupied our haciendas and our village, and claimed all for the government."

Starbuck frowned. "I didn't think the Juarez people ever turned to appropriating—"

"It did not. The Scorpion and his friends have hopes of taking control, and to enable them to do so they gather wealth and strength by such tactics. All was done in their own selfish interest, and of such the true leaders in Mexico City are unaware.

"This fact we knew and so we fought Jaramillo. In the end we lost, for we had no money, few guns, and the peons, except for a small number, feared to aid us. Our parents, our brothers and sisters, our friends and those of us who were captured, were placed before a firing squad and killed as enemies of the state. I was in hiding at the time. So also were Ortega and Vasquez and a handful of others, and thus for a time we were unaware of the massacre.

"Francisco was not so fortunate. He had returned, was attempting to smuggle food to his family, and came upon the executions. Powerless to stay the rifles of the Scorpion's soldiers, he could do nothing but watch. Such has turned him dark and filled him with the death wish."

"Can't see how your government can hold killing a man like Jaramillo against you," Starbuck commented. "Seems to me you've done the country a favor."

Bravo flipped the cigarette butt into the cold ashes of the fire. "It is hard for you to comprehend, senor, this I know. In your United States you have but one government, which is strong and has much power. In my country there is also a central government, in Mexico City, which is patterned after yours, but unfortunately the likeness ends there. It has little strength—and Mexico is a big land.

"There are many cliques, each with its leader who would be a *Presidente*. They have those who follow them, and often among those are men with much influence in our capital; some are actually members of the government. Jaramillo was a part of one such clique. He and those who backed him, because of his ruthlessness, were rapidly becoming very powerful, and word of such success reached others with like ambitions.

"He had made of our village an example of the futility in opposing him, allowing his soldiers to claim the women and girls for their own use, burning all that he could not use of our crops as well as the houses and huts, and was preparing to move his army, which though not large was well equipped and efficient, to a distant town of size.

"This became known and the *alcalde* of that town sought me out. He was a friend of my father's, and while I did not like him because he was a member of another clique, courtesy required that I hear him out. He was the spokesman for such a group, he said, one that had strong ties in Mexico City. They feared the growing strength of the Scorpion and his backers, and knowing what he had done to my parents and those of my friends, had wish to hire us for a certain job."

Shawn nodded. "The job was to kill him."

"Yes. I would be required to select three men whom I could trust. We would each be paid twenty-five hundred dollars in gold for our efforts. A man known to be an expert in such matters, and who had access to Jaramillo, would be the leader and do the planning and make the arrangements. He was known to us only as Amigo, an American, and he would be paid five thousand in gold."

Amigo—the Spanish word for friend. Starbuck's attention sharpened. Could Dominguez be talking about Ben?

"I called upon Carlos and Francisco and Felipe Vasquez to participate in this venture. At first we would not think of taking pay for such; ridding the country of El Escorpion was in itself a reward, but

21

then we thought of what good we could do with so much gold—restore the village, buy many guns with which to arm and fight against the Jaramillos, even hire some of the mercenaries who had deserted the French and remained in Mexico.

"Thus we decided to take the gold, and with it rebuild our lives and those of others who still remained in the Joaquin Valley, and prepare ourselves and them so that never again would we be crushed under the heel of a man such as Jaramillo—"

"Bravo!"

Ortega's sharp voice cut into Dominguez' words. Beyond him Gomez had also appeared at the fringe of the brush, was hurrying toward the horses.

"What is wrong?"

Ortega's reply was a flow of Spanish as he, too, wheeled away. Bravo leaped to his feet.

"The posse comes," he said, facing Shawn. "It is necessary that we leave quickly."

4

Gomez and Ortega were mounted and spurring away by the time Shawn and Dominguez were in the saddle. Swinging in behind Bravo, he followed the vaquero as they raced toward the river. Somewhere in back of them a man shouted; it was evident they had either been seen or heard as they rode out of the coulee.

They came to the Rio Grande, a broad but shallow, somewhat muddy river. At once Carlos veered into a break in the stream's bank, and cut down to the bottom. Willows grew tall in the wet, spongy soil, providing them immediately with an effective screen.

More yells were going up back in the grove, and Gomez, riding in front of Starbuck as they made their way single file along the edge of the swiftly flowing water, turned on his saddle and glanced back, his brown features intent. Bravo, bringing up the rear of the small cavalcade, said something in Spanish to him and he resumed his position, apparently reassured.

Abruptly Ortega drew to a halt, and swinging his horse hard left, bulled a path through the willows into a brush-encircled cove. When all were inside the pocket, Gomez dismounted quietly, careful to create no splash as he stepped into the knee-deep back water, and disappeared downstream. Moments later Shawn saw him climb out onto the bank, and concealed by brush, turn his attention toward the edge of the grove.

Presently the soft thud of approaching horses broke the hush. The posse recruited by the two Mexican agents was drawing near. Bravo placed a finger to his lips, shook his head warningly for silence. Starbuck nodded, began to rub the sorrel's neck to keep him quiet. As for himself he was impatient to ask the vaquero more about the

23

American who had been involved with them in the assassination, the man they called Amigo; but that would have to wait.

There were at least a dozen riders in the party, Shawn guessed. He could not see them all because of the willows and the doveweed and rabbitbush that grew high along the river bank. He could hear them talking back and forth but their words were not clearly audible.

After a time the sound of their passage faded. Francisco Gomez returned from his hiding place, wading slowly across the small pond that floored the cove. He stepped up onto the saddle, making remarks in Spanish to Dominguez and Ortega as he did, and then pulling his horse about, struck back upstream.

"Francisco says that many of those in the posse believe we have crossed the river, returned to Mexico. Sandoval and Pacheco do not," Bravo explained as they moved on.

"That means they'll likely be back."

"Without doubt. But they did not find the camp. We can remain there again for a time."

They reached the cut in the Rio Grande's bank, climbed back up to the higher ground. At once Gomez spurred off in the direction in which the search party had ridden.

"He will see for a certainty that no one tries to trick us," Bravo said as they moved into the trees and pointed for the coulee.

Once again dismounted and the sorrel secure, Starbuck resumed his seat on the log in the small clearing and glanced expectantly at Dominguez. The vaquero was speaking rapidly to Ortega in Spanish, seemingly trying to convince, or perhaps reassure, him of something. Abruptly Carlos pivoted and stalked off into the brush.

Bravo swung his attention to Starbuck. Lifting his hands, he let them fall to his sides in an expression of helplessness.

"I fear you have no friend in Carlos, senor."

"Be a lot easier if you'd call me by my front name, Shawn. . . . Why?"

Dominguez nodded, smiled. "It will be an honor. . . . He thinks all Americans are untrustworthy and bring bad luck. He believes it is your fault the Assassins, as he calls Pacheco and Sandoval, and their searching party came near to finding us."

"My fault! How the hell does he figure—"

"You will pardon him, please. He has thought such for a long time. There is something in the past of which he does not speak, a bitter experience no doubt."

"Can think of a few Mexicans that I wouldn't trust very far either. It works both ways."

"That is true. All Americans are not bad, just as all Mexicans are not good. But that is something Carlos cannot admit. . . . Do you wish to hear the remainder of our story, which is now our problem?"

25

Starbuck nodded. He also wanted to know more of Amigo but it had occurred to him that it would be wise to let the subject come up naturally and make no issue of it until he was sure of his ground. He had the feeling that Amigo was no friend of the vaqueros.

"All went well," Bravo began, again taking out his tobacco and sheaf of brown papers, offering them first to Shawn who declined as before, and then fell to thoughtfully rolling himself a smoke. "Amigo was, as we had been told, one of experience in such matters. He arranged for us to be in a nearby village where the Scorpion had established new headquarters after destroying Escobar. Under a pretext we were escorted into his presence, and then at a signal from Amigo we turned upon Jaramillo and the officers with him. All were quickly slain.

"It was Francisco himself who drove his blade into the throat of El Escorpion, and then so that all would share equally in the deed the rest of us plunged our knives into his body.

"But a peon chancing to pass by saw and gave the alarm, and as we made the attempt to escape we encountered a company of Jaramillo's soldiers returning from a raid on another village. Felipe Vasquez was killed during the engagement, and finally, to save our lives, we were forced to disband and flee separately.

"It was first agreed among us, however, that we

would meet in seven days at the Cantina de Toros, a saloon in Juarez. Amigo would report the success of the mission to the men who hired us, and collect the gold. When we met in Juarez on the seventh day we each would receive our share.

"And so it was. One by one we came to the cantina—first Gomez, then Ortega, and then I—but there was no Amigo. It was necessary that we use great care while we waited, for we knew that Sandoval and Pacheco, who work for those that backed the Scorpion and his friends, were already seeking us.

"Those friends of his in Mexico City had strong ties with certain high-up members of the government and thus were able to obtain papers for Sandoval and Pacheco and make it appear that they are of authority and truly agents of the government. Such credentials made it possible for them to enlist aid wherever they chose to present them, as you have witnessed.

"Therefore, all inquiring and searching for Amigo on our part was necessarily done secretly and with great care, but finally we did learn from a relative of a friend who had become acquainted with Amigo that he had come to Juarez several days early, and that his pockets were heavy with gold."

"But he had skipped, left you and the others holding the bag," Shawn finished in a disgusted tone.

Bravo frowned, smiled uncertainly. "I am not

sure of your meaning. Such an expression was not taught where I learned my English."

"He ran off with your part of the money."

"That is right, but we did not know this at once. We still had hope that a reason, perhaps the presence of Sandoval and Pacheco, had caused Amigo to flee Juarez, seek safety in El Paso where he would be awaiting us.

"Consequently we crossed the river one night and began our search again. This time I was required to do so alone. Carlos and Francisco were seen that first day by the Assassins and barely escaped from them."

"Lucky I wasn't around, or Ortega would be blaming that on me," Starbuck murmured.

"It is likely," Bravo said, smiling. "But to Amigo. I learned that he was seen in the Longhorn Saloon, the place where I met you. After asking many questions I discovered that he was there but a short time, during which he gambled and drank much, spending gold freely. And then he departed."

Bravo's accounting ended abruptly, flatly. Shawn glanced up at the vaquero, now studying the tip of his cold cigarette.

"That it? This Amigo just rode off?"

"That is it," Bravo said with a shrug. He turned his head to watch Ortega reentering the coulee. "With all of the gold he has gone—leaving us to hold the bag, as you have said."

"How long ago was that?"

"A week perhaps, possibly a day or two more. The bartender could not recall and be exact."

Ortega had crossed to the horses, removed his saddlebags, and was rummaging about inside, probably for something to eat as it was near the usual hour. On beyond him Francisco Gomez was loping slowly across the grassy flat toward the coulee.

"The bartender have any idea where Amigo was heading for?"

"North, to a town of which I have heard. I had returned to the saloon to talk further with him about such when Pacheco and Sandoval came. The rest is of knowledge to you as you were there and have been with us since that time on."

Shawn nodded, absently following the movements of Gomez with unseeing eyes as he rode into the clearing and halted at its far edge. Could Ben be guilty of such deceit—of so heartless a double-cross?

"This man Amigo," he asked quietly after a time, "was that just what you called him or is it his name?"

5

Dominguez stroked his clipped moustache uncertainly. Ortega half turned, scowled over a shoulder.

"His name does not matter," he said in English as perfect as Bravo's. "He is a thief, a man who is not a man, a dog that we should have never trusted."

Sweat was standing out in large beads on the forehead of the Mexican, and his dark skin had a shine to it.

"It would have been better had I listened to my heart and slit his belly."

"We would then have never gotten the gold, Carlos," Bravo said heavily.

"Why not? Would they not have paid you or me or Francisco?"

"It was arranged that the gold would be handed to Amigo since it was he who was in charge."

"Because they did not trust us, no doubt!" Ortega snapped. "They trust him because he is an American. They mistrust us because we are only Mexicans."

"It was an arrangement that we agreed upon," Dominguez insisted quietly.

"One we should have known better than to accept! It is well proven that no American can be trusted with gold. Is that not so?"

Gomez, standing at the side of his horse listening, crossed to Ortega, dropped a hand on the man's broad shoulder.

"Do not excite yourself, old friend," he said, also speaking in English. "All will come out for the best."

"No!" Ortega shouted, knocking the vaquero's hand aside. "We have lost all! We have nothing now—we will have nothing in the days to come—all because we have put our trust in a gringo dog!"

Starbuck, silent through the tirade, rose involuntarily. Dominguez shook his head, eyes beseeching. Shawn settled back on the log.

"You sound a fool, Carlos," Bravo said in a mild tone, "for only a fool could have such thoughts. Starbuck here is our friend—and there have been other Americans who were not false."

Ortega spat. "Fool or no, I will not again put my faith in any of them. I am finished with Americans."

There was silence after that. Ortega, a strip of jerky in his hand, ripped the dried meat into two pieces, handed one to Gomez, and dropped to his haunches. Francisco squatted beside him. Bravo studied them briefly and then turned away, faced Shawn.

"You ask of Amigo. Such was all he was ever called and the name by which he was made known to us. Why? Does it have meaning for you?"

Shawn thought quickly. If Amigo was Ben and the vaqueros had information as to where he could be found, it would be important that he get there first; Carlos Ortega, and probably Bravo and Gomez, would have but one purpose in mind—to kill him. He shrugged indifferently.

"Know a man named Damon Friend. There's a chance he's the one you're talking about. . . . What'd he look like?"

Bravo glanced questioningly at his friends. Gomez said, "Like you, perhaps—like other

31

Americans. To me you Americans all look much the same."

Shawn smiled faintly. That could mean anything—and nothing. "There maybe something special about him, like a scar? What color were his hair and his eyes?"

Ortega, his jaw set, got slowly to his feet. "What is this, gringo?" he demanded suspiciously. "Can this Amigo be a friend of yours—a partner?"

"Don't be a damned fool!" Starbuck snarled, finally out of patience. "Just trying to give you a little help."

Amigo could be his brother, he was forced to admit. It seemed likely the fifth member of the assassination party would have been referred to by another name during their time together, and since such had apparently not been the case, the possibility was strong that the man was Ben going under his assumed name of Friend. Too, Ben had dropped out of sight and remained so for several months. Being somewhere in Mexico would explain that.

Shawn became aware of Bravo's close attention, faced him inquiringly.

"Something you want to say?"

Dominguez nodded. "There is this meaning in your words—that you would help us find Amigo?"

"No reason why I can't. Not doing anything special. Was about to head north myself."

"Why would you do this for us?" Ortega said, his voice still weighted with suspicion. "There is no reason for such unless you expect part of the gold for pay. . . . I for one will not—"

"Forget the gold," Shawn cut in flatly.

"You have no interest in such? Hah! That is difficult to believe."

"I'd be a fool if I said I didn't. Just about any man you'll come across has use for gold, but it's not my reason for offering to help."

"What is this reason, senor?" Gomez asked in his quiet way.

"Already said it—heading north myself. Since you'll be strangers, and I know the country, I figure I can give you a hand."

Ortega shook his head stubbornly. "This I do not believe. There is another reason, *Americano*, and I will hear it first before I ride one mile with you."

"Up to you," Starbuck said indifferently.

Bravo spoke sharply in Spanish to Ortega, who then turned away, shoulders stirring slightly, and began to chew on his meat. Gomez, too, resumed his eating. After a moment Dominguez moved to Shawn's side, took a place next to him on the log.

"It would be a favor of great worth to us if you will do this."

"Easily done. I'm going that way—north, and that's the direction the bartender told you Amigo took. Best you know now that it won't be easy for you to get around—even with me along. Mexicans aren't welcome in some parts of my country, the same as Americans find no friends in certain places in Mexico."

"Of such I have been told. Also, it is likely that Sandoval and Pacheco would soon be on our trail. They are devils that cannot be lost once they have begun the hunt."

"They'll have papers authorizing them to be in this country—and you won't. That'll cause you some trouble if you run into a nosy lawman."

"Nosy?"

"Curious—"

"I see. Could you save us from such?"

"Maybe not save you, once they picked you up. Thing to do is avoid getting in such a tight spot."

"And you expect no reward for these services?"

"Hell, no!" Shawn said wearily, brushing at the sweat on his face. "Not saying I wouldn't like to meet with this Amigo, see if he's Damon Friend—but mainly I'll be doing it as a favor. Didn't you ever do a man a good turn just to be doing it?"

Dominguez lowered his head. "Of course, good friend. I apologize for not understanding, just as I apologize also for Carlos. We have been so long living with evil and mistrust that we have forgotten what it is to be among honest men, I fear. It is with many thanks that we accept your offer."

Shawn threw a glance at Ortega. "What about him?"

Bravo's shoulders stirred. "He will be difficult

and I beg of you to have patience. I shall talk to him."

"Maybe you'd best hash . . . I mean talk it over before we do any more planning."

"Such will not be necessary. I see that it is most important we have someone such as yourself with us—one who can guide us to the place where I believe Amigo has gone."

Starbuck looked up in surprise. "You know the name of the town?"

"Only from things—from words—told us and others by him many times when we were together. Often he mentioned that with the gold he would receive he had a plan to open for himself a saloon where gambling could be done. A trail town, he called it, where men could gather after the cattle had been driven to the stockyards, and spend their money."

"Can think of quite a few trail towns. He ever mention a name?"

"Yes, and it was repeated by him to the bartender of the Longhorn Saloon, a fact told me shortly before Sandoval and Pacheco came this morning. It was for this place that Amigo said he was riding."

"A streak of good luck for us if he meant it. What was the name of the town?"

"Dodge City," Dominguez answered.

6

Starbuck gave that thought. "Long way from here. Two weeks steady riding, maybe more. You pretty sure that's where he was going?"

Bravo's shoulders stirred.

"Could've just mentioned Dodge City so's to throw you off the trail," Shawn continued. "Specially if he had it in mind all the time to beat you out of your share."

"It is possible," Dominguez agreed, "but we do not think so. He has told us of this Dodge City before."

Shawn was still not convinced. "Still could have been part of a plan he had, like I've said."

"I do not think there was such a plan. Carlos does not agree with me on that, but to me it is most likely. When we encountered the company of El Escorpion's soldiers and there was much fighting, it looked very desperate for us all. Felipe was then killed and I myself began to despair of seeing another sunrise. Only then was it that we agreed to separate and each seek an escape for himself. I think Amigo believed we all were killed in our attempts and that he alone survived."

"You have a woman's kind heart, Bravo," Ortega said wearily. "If such were true you can be sure the gringo had it all arranged for us to die. Since we did not, it is plain that he simply stole the gold for himself."

Dominguez sighed heavily. "Well, no matter. He has what is ours and we shall have it."

"To be paid for killing El Escorpion was not necessary," Gomez said. "It was a task I would have gladly accepted with no thought of pay."

"And I," Ortega added. "This Amigo was not needed."

"You cannot believe that, Carlos," Bravo said. "To accomplish it required much organization and bribery for which we were not equipped, and he was. But to be rewarded for killing Jaramillo, I agree, was unnecessary. It is a little like being paid to make love to a beautiful woman. Such pay is not necessary, but since it is offered, it is accepted.

"And since, in this case, payment was suggested we would be fools not to take it, for it opens up a future of sorts to us—and others. We can make a new beginning—"

"It is a dream, *compadre*," Ortega cut in. "We are wanted criminals in Mexico. There is no future for us except one of running and hiding—and finally death."

"You have changed your mind about returning to the Joaquin Valley and rebuilding our homes?" Bravo asked.

"I am not one to fool myself. Our way of living has come to an end. The time of the *hacendado* and the *peon* as we knew it is over, and I for one care not for what lies ahead. I have seen all of this life that I care to, and when I have evened the score for the evil dealt me, I shall be ready to leave it. Is that not your feeling, too, Francisco?"

Gomez raised his eyes, stared off across the river at the barren, ragged mountains of Mexico, dull gray in the shimmering heat.

"To die is nothing. It is the easy way to answer all questions. But I make no plans for the future, either. What comes with the sunrise I shall meet and conquer, or be conquered. . . . Is that not a wise philosophy, gringo?"

Shawn grinned. Somehow there was no sting to the term as it was being applied to him by Francisco. It seemed only an affectionate nickname.

"Good as any, I reckon, but I always figured there was more to life than that."

"Only because you have never lived through a raid by El Escorpion and his soldiers," Gomez said, his features going taut. "You have not seen his butchery, nor heard the screams of women and children, or watched your family murdered by men who laughed, or seen the flames destroy your heritage and all that was dear to you!"

Francisco's voice had risen to a fevered pitch. "You are right," Starbuck said, seeking to relieve the vaquero's torment. "I can't judge something that hasn't happened to me."

"May God spare you from such," Gomez said, his voice again at normal level. Getting to his feet, he turned away. "It is best we watch the road."

Silent, Starbuck watched the Mexican move off into the brush. Somewhere in the distance a dog was barking, and below them along the river children's voices could be heard, remote and hollow, as they played along the banks of the Rio Grande.

"It is no longer safe to remain here," Bravo said, breaking the hush. "Sandoval and Pacheco will return and we should be gone."

"I am ready," Ortega said. "Do we go north with this *Americano*?"

Starbuck stiffened. The term was an epithet when Carlos employed it, and it grated on his nerves.

"If he wishes to accompany us, I think it will be to our advantage," Dominguez said, glancing at Shawn. "No doubt there is much trouble we can avoid if we have his guidance."

Ortega shook his head, spat, released a torrent of scornful Spanish. It had to do with him, Starbuck knew. He turned at once to Bravo.

"Like to know what he said."

Dominguez frowned, hesitated briefly. Then, "Only that it is possible you will lead us into a trap if there is profit in such for you. As I have said, he is suspicious of all Americans."

"Up to him—he can think what he wants, but you tell him for me that hereafter if he's got anything to say about me, to have guts enough to speak in English so I can understand—else keep his mouth shut!"

There was no need for Bravo to translate. Ortega understood. Half turned from Starbuck, he listened intently, and when it was said, he came about slowly. His small, dark eyes were narrowed, and his mouth a hard, straight line.

"Very well, gringo, so will it be. But take heed, the day will come when we shall see which of us has the most courage."

"Not interested in proving that or anything else, on your part or mine," Shawn retorted, and swung his attention to Bravo. "I'm ready to pull out anytime."

Dominguez glanced at the sun. "The day is well started—"

"Doesn't matter. There's a town called Las Cruces up the river a piece. Can probably make it to there by dark if we push the horses."

"And from there?"

"Keep going right on up the valley, and then across a mesa to Santa Fe. That'll be the easiest route. Once we get that far we cut through the mountains for the Indian Territory and then into Kansas."

"Kansas? That is the state where Dodge City is?"

"Yeah. Once we've crossed the line it's about a three-day ride."

"You have not yet explained why you will do this favor for us."

It was Ortega again. Starbuck shrugged in weary resignation. "All right, I'll give you a reason since you don't seem to savvy a good turn when it's offered. . . . I want to meet this man you call Amigo, see if he's one I know as Damon Friend."

"I see. This Damon Friend—he owes you something?"

Starbuck smiled faintly. "Yes, guess you can say he does. That satisfy you?"

Ortega nodded. "It is a reason I can understand."

Starbuck mopped at the sweat on his face. The heat in the vast, gray rock bowl in which lay El Paso and its sister city of Juarez was intense and mounting even higher. If Bravo and the others decided they would delay their departure until later for some reason, he'd go on ahead. It would be much cooler up the river away from the sun-seared mountains that rimmed the area.

"It has been a time since you met with this man Damon Friend?" Ortega continued.

"Of what difference is that, Carlos?" Bravo demanded, suddenly out of patience. "You are like an old woman with your stupid questions! To me, and now to you, Shawn has explained that he knows of a man named Friend. He is curious to know if he is the same as Amigo. Permit the matter to drop there. Are you agreeable?"

Ortega's thick shoulders lifted, fell. Staring at Bravo for a long moment, he said, "It is agreed," and shifted his attention to Gomez, who appeared abruptly at the edge of the coulee.

Francisco's features were strained as he strode

toward the horses. "It is best we move again. I have the feeling of danger."

Bravo nodded. "We have just decided to do so and were about to call you. We ride north."

"Good," Gomez said, vaulting onto his saddle. "Perhaps it will be possible to leave the Assassins far behind."

"You, too, are a dreamer, Francisco," Ortega said as he and the others hurried to mount up. "Those two are the same as death; one can never escape."

7

Bravo Dominguez, swaying gently with the rocking motion of his horse as they loped steadily along the banks of the Rio Grande, cast a side glance at Starbuck.

The American sat easily and naturally on his saddle, seemed actually a part of his big sorrel gelding. A bit hard to understand, this one, but he guessed it was because he and the others had been out of touch with honorable men for so long.

Shawn was not very far along in years, Bravo supposed; perhaps a year or two younger than himself. He'd turned twenty-five his last birthday. *Last birthday!* It had been far different from those in the past; it had been spent hiding in a cave in the Las Madres mountains, without food or water—not to mention the heat. The abode of the devil could have been no hotter!

Shawn was what his father would have termed a *vagabundo*—a drifter—but he would not have meant it in the sense of the American being a lazy, shiftless tramp, but a wanderer experiencing all that life had to offer.

There were many such men. Some were beset by fate and cast adrift for one reason or another; others were seekers, persons who roamed ceaselessly in search of something—gold, fame, to forget a woman, to find one, or to only satisfy a craving to see what they had not before laid eyes upon.

The latter, Bravo decided, seemed to fit Shawn best of all reasons—a man who simply traveled, and the look of one who had been many places and seen much was stamped clearly upon him.

He had that long, lean appearance of a lone wolf. His eyes were deep set, a pale gray that at times, as when he had been angered slightly by Carlos, took on a sharp fierceness as they peered out from his shelf of brows. He could handle himself well, too, such being evident in the saloon when Pacheco and Sandoval had started trouble. That he wore his gun low on his left hip, that the holster was thonged to his leg, were not merely for show. This Shawn Starbuck was a *pistolero* and undoubtedly one of excellence, he was certain.

There was also the matter of the belt buckle he wore—a silver square with engraving and the figure of a man posed ready to fight with his clenched fists. That had to mean something, also. After becoming better acquainted he'd ask about it. At this point in their relationship to do so would be impolite.

Twisting about, Bravo glanced at Gomez, raised his brows questioningly. Francisco shook his head indicating that so far there had been no sign of their being followed by the two agents, but that was neither proof nor guarantee. The area through which they were traveling was so overgrown with trees and brush that visibility was severely restricted and it was not possible to see anyone even within a near distance.

He would not worry about it, however; Francisco's ability to detect the approach of danger was amazing. Some sort of sixth sense operated within him, warned him of trouble, and to that very moment had never failed. Strangely, it was a faculty that he had not possessed until after that terrible day when his family had met death.

Again Bravo looked ahead. The land along the river was rich, would offer much to a man who might wish to work it. And the great cottonwood trees—some were as thick through as a man was tall, and could no doubt spread their deep shade over his father's entire hacienda and patio, were it still standing and not mere rubble.

It had been a fine place to grow up—all the gentle politeness of old Spain, the practical hard-headedness of Mexico. Culture, refinement, the art

44

of being a gentleman, the need to be honest, hard working—he'd found it all there just as had Carlos and Felipe Vasquez and Francisco and many others on the sprawling estates of their fathers.

And to a man all had lost. Every one of the old haciendas in the Joaquin Valley that had weathered bandits, Indian raids, revolutions, drought, flood, and all other conceivable hardships were now gone, their proud owners dead or in hiding, the peons who worked for them scattered, supposedly free but likely starving in their newly acquired state of liberty.

He hoped that upon returning to the valley with ample gold he would be able to seek them out, restore them to their customary status. They had been totally dependent upon his father, and without *patron* to see that they were properly fed, clothed, and had a place to sleep, they faced want.

And such could be accomplished, and a measure of security established for them, with the gold that Amigo was keeping from him and his two companions. With it a semblance of the old days could be reestablished, and measures could be taken to safeguard all from such as the Scorpion.

Bravo Dominguez frowned, rubbed at his chin as he gave that thought. Both Carlos and Francisco, who had agreed with him earlier on such a plan, now appeared to be having doubts as to its practicability. Well, let them waver; once Shawn Starbuck had conducted them to Dodge City, and

45

their gold was recovered from Amigo, he would talk with them, make them see that it was something that they must do.

Perhaps it would even be possible to persuade Shawn to join with them.

Starbuck raised himself in the stirrups and threw his glance as far ahead as possible. They should be nearing Las Cruces. Sundown was not far off, and using it as his gauge it would seem they should be reaching the settlement.

Although he could see nothing but the tree-crowded flat that bordered the river, he had noted several small farms back against the foothills and that stirred a recollection within him; they had been just outside the town, he thought, and if so Las Cruces could be only a mile or so in the distance. Turning, he nodded to Bravo.

"Expect we're about there."

The vaquero smiled, brushed at his face. "That is good to hear, *compadre*. The saddle grows harder when the belly is empty."

Shawn nodded. "I figure we'd best play it smart here, being so close to El Paso and your two agent friends—"

"To call them friends—" Dominguez began, missing entirely the oblique meaning Starbuck had in mind, "I—"

Shawn grinned. "Not exactly how I intended for that to sound to you. What I'm saying is that we should be careful. Best you keep out of sight—dressed the way you are. I'll go into town, buy trail supplies myself."

"I understand. . . . It is your plan to spend the night here?"

"Yes. Got to get ourselves set and this'll be the only town close where we can. Besides trail grub, we'll need to get blankets, cartridges, canteens, and the like. Pretty well fixed myself with the outfit I've lugged along for years. It's you and the others I'm thinking about."

"True, there are things we must have," the Mexican said, motioning at Ortega and Gomez as he spoke. "We have lived with little, since it was necessary to move often, and at times quickly. After being paid by Amigo we expected to buy many things we needed, but since there was no payment such did not come to pass. . . . I shall talk with my *compadres* and learn what it is they have need of. Also I will collect from them what money they possess in order to pay for what will be needed. I fear, however, they will have little if any silver or gold."

Starbuck scratched at his jaw. He hadn't given any thought to the possibility that his traveling companions might be broke. He was none too flush himself, and it had been his intention, once he got back in cattle country, to find a job for the remainder of the summer, possibly through the winter if the pay was good.

But he reckoned he could manage; he had a few dollars—two double-eagles and a bit of silver, he recalled—and if the vaqueros were unable to come up with any cash he'd have enough to get the party by.

It would be worth it and more if this Amigo turned out to be Ben. The chances that the two men were one and the same seemed good, although he did not like to think that his own brother could have sunk so low as to become a cheat and a thief. Participating in a plot to assassinate a man like Jaramillo was understandable, but to beat his partners out of their share of a promised fee, that didn't seem likely—not if he could judge from what little he had learned of Ben in the past.

But conditions alter men; Ben could have changed. He could have experienced a long, hard run of bad luck that turned him about, gave him a different set of values from those their father and mother had drilled into them when they were boys growing up. Such was nothing new, and it could have happened to him.

As far as he knew, his brother's last good job was the one he'd held as a guard for the Skull Mining people in Wickenburg, Arizona Territory. Misfortune and fate had combined to deprive him of it, and it was not long after that he had dropped out of sight.

He could have gotten wind of the Jaramillo deal then, or possibly been approached by someone who knew him and offered him five thousand in gold to head up the assassination party, and being down and out, possibly he had accepted.

"Bravo—"

Francisco Gomez' voice was tense, husky. Shawn wheeled, cut back to Dominguez' side.

"What is it?"

"I hear many horses," Francisco replied. "They come from the way of El Paso. It is my belief that it is the *Asesinos*, who bring with them what the American will call a posse."

Bravo turned his taut features to Starbuck. "It is best we heed the warning. What Francisco feels is always in the end a fact."

"Then we'll get out of here fast," Shawn replied. "Which way?"

Starbuck gave it a moment's thought. Then, "Straight through town. Follow me close."

8

Grim set, in a tight group, they entered the town— a church, the Amador Hotel, a score or so of squat, flat-roofed houses, Lindeman's General Store, three or four saloons, a livery stable—all set back a short distance from the river. Riding at a lope, they traveled down its one street, never slowing, making it evident they were in flight.

Reaching the trees beyond the clearing in which the settlement lay, and short of a second village that Shawn recalled stood nearby, he pulled the party to a halt in the dense grove.

"Road we're on goes on up the river," he explained. "Next big town's Socorro—about a three-day ride. Was the way I'd figured for us to go, but with Pacheco and Sandoval and whoever they've got with them on our heels, it's best we make a change."

"But we must go north—to Santa Fe," Bravo protested.

"Up the valley's the easiest route, but it's not the only one," Starbuck replied, pointing to an irregular formation of spired hills to the east. "We can cut through the Organ Mountains, keep on their other side. If we're lucky the posse'll fall for our trick and think we kept right on going up the valley."

Dominguez glanced at Gomez and Carlos Ortega, nodded smilingly. "It is understood now why we ride through the town in view of all. When asked by the Assassins, a man would say yes that four riders passed that way in much hurry."

"What I'm hoping. Meanwhile, best we cut across to those trees near that hill and pull up. Be a good place to lay low until we see if the Assassins take the bait."

He was applying to Sandoval and Pacheco the same term as did the vaqueros, thereby accepting their version of the Jaramillo incident, Shawn realized, as well as their explanation of the true identities of the two Mexican agents. He reckoned it didn't matter now, anyway; he had declared himself there in El Paso's Longhorn Saloon when he had chosen to stand by Bravo Dominguez, and right or wrong, he was now thoroughly involved.

They pounded across to the upper grove of trees, doubled back through it toward Las Cruces for a mile or so, pulled up finally in a small, cleared pocket at the foot of a low butte screened from view by a wall of mesquite and other rank growth.

"Camp here till morning—unless that posse gets wise and starts poking around," Starbuck said as they dismounted. "Don't figure they will, however. Expect it'll be sometime tomorrow before they find out we're not in the valley ahead of them."

"And tomorrow we will continue, eh?" Ortega said.

There was a thread of doubt in the Mexican's voice, as if he anticipated their being abandoned at this point. Shawn curbed his temper, turned his attention to the distant mountains. The last of the day's sun still shone upon the jagged formations, highlighting the spires, which looked much like the pipes of a gigantic organ.

"Can bet on it," he said quietly. Then, "Need to be stocking up for the trail—grub mostly. Be days when we won't be anywhere near a town so we need to go well fixed. You want to leave it up to me?"

Dominguez shrugged. "What is satisfactory to

you also will be to us. You go to Las Cruces to make the purchase?"

"Only me," Starbuck said. "Don't want any of you showing yourselves."

"But what of you? Is there not danger that someone will recall your having passed through with us?"

"Aim to be careful. It'll be dark, and that'll help. Chance I have to take, anyway. Got to have supplies."

Bravo said, "It is so, but to buy we must have money. I fear I have but a few centavos in Mexican money. How is it with you, Francisco?"

Gomez thrust his hands into his pockets, withdrew them palms spread to show that he had nothing. Slipping a ring off a finger, he offered it to Starbuck.

"This is of gold, senor. It will buy an amount of cash."

Shawn glanced at it, guessed that it was family jewelry since it bore a crest. Ortega stepped up, belt knife extended hilt forward.

"I have only this—and my pistol," he said. "The pistol I must keep, but for my share I will pay."

Starbuck shook his head, handed back the bit of jewelry and brushed aside the knife. "Got no use for the ring," he said, and reaching down drew his own blade from inside his left boot, displayed it. "Or a knife either. You can settle up with me when you get your gold from Amigo."

Bravo and Francisco nodded. Ortega, face sullen, slid the weapon back into its sheath. "I want no favor from you, *Americano*," he said, turning away. "Later I will pay. Of that you can be certain."

"He is grateful," Dominguez murmured in a low voice. "He cannot admit it to you, but it is so."

"Forget it," Starbuck replied, and glanced to the west. The glow beyond the horizon was fading and full darkness was only minutes away. Crossing to the sorrel, he stepped to the saddle. "I'll head into town now. There anything special you need—bullets, maybe?"

Bravo exchanged questioning looks with the others, faced Shawn. He smiled ruefully. "It is strange, but we are well prepared for death, have nothing to sustain life. I suppose it is a sign of our time."

Starbuck shrugged at the paradox, and keeping to the brush and trees, rode to the settlement.

Night had closed in and lamps had been lit in the stores and houses when he swung into the street and angled through the loose dust for the rear of the general store. The sorrel would be well hidden from sight there; it was best he take no chances on the big gelding being recognized by someone who had noticed them riding through.

Circling the squat structure, he entered, found no one there other than the owner—a short, paunchy man with a fringe of reddish hair encircling a bald pate. This would be Lindeman, he supposed, recalling the sign on the front of the building.

"Something I can do for you, friend?"

"Need some grub," Starbuck replied, aware that he must be careful and arouse no suspicion by purchasing an unusually large amount of food for one man. "Expect to be on the trail for quite a spell—and I'm a big eater, so you'd best figure heavy."

Lindeman bobbed. "You got a list or you want me to use my own judgment?"

"Leaving it up to you," Shawn said, and pivoting, sauntered toward the doorway. A half a dozen riders were moving down the street toward the hotel.

The storekeeper, beginning to assemble items on the counter, glanced up. "Posse—from El Paso," he explained. "Guess they're quitting for the night."

Starbuck, careful to keep out of the direct light, studied the party more closely. Besides Sandoval and Pacheco there were now four soldiers—two American and two wearing the uniform of the Mexican army. The agents had been able to recruit help from both sides of the border.

"Who they chasing?"

"Bunch of renegades," Lindeman answered. "Three Mexicans and an American. Claim they murdered some highfalutin general."

"They supposed to be around here?"

"Rode through town about dark, heading up the

54

river. Expect the posse'll eat and rest a spell, then take out after them again."

"They figure they're somewhere in the valley, that it?"

"Yeah. Was the way they was going when they went through here. . . . Reckon this'll take care of what you'll be needing. Ain't much variety but there's plenty of the stuff that'll stick to your ribs."

Shawn watched the posse pull in behind the hotel and disappear into the shadows. Wheeling, he returned to the counter. Lindeman was putting the supplies into a pair of flour sacks and tying strings about the necks.

"Can hang these on your pack horse like saddlebags," he said. "Sacks are tight wove. Won't be no dust getting in."

Shawn handed a gold piece to the storekeeper, gave brief consideration to obtaining a pack animal. One would relieve the horses, there was little doubt of that, but it would also slow them down—and if it became necessary to make a long, fast run they could be forced to abandon the horse, supplies and all. He dismissed the thought, and pocketing his change, slung the sacks of groceries over his shoulder and started for the door.

"You say you was heading west?" the storekeeper called after him.

"Don't recollect saying, but that's a pretty good guess," Starbuck said. "Always had a liking for Tucson."

"Ain't never been there myself but I hear tell it's a mighty fine little town."

Tucson was west, and south; as well not correct the conclusion to which the merchant had jumped concerning his supposed destination, in the event the Assassins, failing to find him and the vaqueros in the valley, doubled back and began asking questions.

"Well good luck to you—and I'm obliged for the business. . . . There's a good reward out for them renegades if you sight them."

Shawn nodded. He paused in the doorway and threw his glance toward the Amador. Two men were standing at the hotel's side entrance. He gave them close scrutiny, saw that they were not Pacheco or Sandoval and that neither wore a uniform, and stepped quickly into the open.

Circling the store building, Starbuck retraced his steps to the sorrel and mounted. Then, well in the deep shadows, he followed out a line of trees until he was clear of the town. Once certain that he would not be seen, he cut back toward the low foothills and returned to the butte.

Bravo and Gomez greeted him as he rode in, Francisco at once taking charge of the sorrel. Ortega, squatting beside the small, protected fire built in a pocket of rocks, merely glanced up.

"There was no trouble?" Dominguez asked. "More time was taken by you than expected."

"No trouble," Shawn replied, laying the sacks of

groceries on a nearby stump. Motioning to Gomez to bring his saddlebags, in which he had a spider, a can for making coffee, and other necessary utensils, he began to dig about in the supplies for food that would provide a good meal. He was hungry and realized that the vaqueros were likely more so than he.

"Did see Pacheco and Sandoval," he said. "Got themselves some soldiers—two of yours and two Americans."

Ortega had come to his feet, frowning darkly. Gomez paused in the act of adding more wood to the fire, while Bravo muttered something in Spanish.

"They are in Las Cruces?" he asked.

"Rode in while I was there. Been up the valley a way, I guess, and when they didn't spot us, decided to come back and rest and get some grub—leastwise, that's what the storekeeper figured. . . . They've put up a reward for us."

"Will they stay the night?"

"Anybody's guess. Storekeeper seemed to think they'd head on out in a while. All depends on how beat their horses are, I expect."

Bravo's shoulders stirred. "Sandoval will not want to delay. He will begin the search for us again soon. Is it not best we ride on? If there is a reward many men will join the hunt—"

"Don't think it's necessary," Starbuck said, drawing his knife and beginning to slice bacon from the side that Lindeman had included. "We're pretty well hid. Be smarter to rest the horses, let them graze and water while we get a good meal under our belts and catch up on sleep, then pull out before daylight."

Gomez had found potatoes in one of the sacks, was slicing several into thin strips in order that they would cook more rapidly. He grinned at Shawn, a pleased look on his brown face.

"It has been many days since we had good food—only scraps."

"Figured that," Starbuck said, setting the skillet over the flames and reaching for one of the canteens. "Can stand some grub myself. We all pitch in, it won't take but a few minutes to get it ready."

Bravo at once began to assist Francisco, taking up an onion, peeling it and dicing it into the skillet with the bacon. Shawn glanced up at Ortega, held the sack of coffee beans toward him.

"Can make the coffee—"

The big vaquero did not move, simply stared back in cold silence. Abruptly he wheeled and started toward the end of the butte.

"Carlos!" Bravo called sharply.

Ortega paused, came half around, a stream of Spanish pouring from his lips. Finished, he continued on. Shawn watched him fade into the shadows, and then fell himself to crushing the coffee beans and dumping the fragments into the small muslin sack he used for confining the grounds.

"Like to know what Ortega said."

Dominguez, finished with the onions, was stirring up a batter of cornmeal to be baked in the spider after the stew was ready.

"It was nothing of importance—"

"Still like to hear it."

Bravo paused, wagged his head slowly. "It is sad that there is so much hate in Carlos. He was saying that because there is now money offered by the Assassins for us, there is less reason than ever to trust you. He has gone to keep watch should you have arranged it with them to follow you back to our camp."

A gust of anger rolled through Starbuck. Raising his eyes, he looked off into the darkness that had swallowed the vaquero, his jaw hard-set, eyes narrowed.

"I think Ortega and me are going to have us a little understanding before long," he said in a low, quiet voice, and resumed the chore of making coffee.

9

The meal over, Shawn made preparations for the long trip ahead by rearranging and distributing their supplies in such a way that no one of the horses would be overburdened. While he was thus occupied, Bravo and Francisco led the animals to water, taking the opportunity to refill their canteens at the same time. Ortega, returning to camp only long enough to eat his food in stolid silence, had resumed his post as self-appointed guard over the trail that led to Las Cruces.

The necessary work done, Starbuck spread his blanket on the smooth ground and stretched out wearily. It had been a long, hard day and tomorrow would be equally trying. Nearby, Gomez and Dominguez also laid their beds, both expressing their relief as they sprawled on the woolen cloth.

"Ortega—he going to sit out there all night?" Shawn wondered. "Ought to get some sleep."

Bravo tossed a handful of wood into the lowering fire. "Carlos is not one to listen."

"He should. Could be need for him to be wide awake tomorrow. Dozing at the wrong time's cost many a man his life."

"When he is tired he will sleep," Francisco said. "That is his way."

Shawn looked off toward the end of the butte. The vaquero had climbed to a higher point, was now a hunched silhouette against the star-studded sky. Off in the trees along the river an owl hooted its lonely question.

"He really think I'd sell you out to Sandoval and Pacheco?"

Bravo's shoulders moved slightly. "Carlos is a brave and honorable man but sometimes he is as a child who does not understand clearly."

"He believes we should run no more from the

Asesinos," Gomez said. "We have talked much of this. It is his contention that it would be better to wait along the trail and kill them."

"Idea might've worked in Mexico," Starbuck said dryly. "Here it'll be a quick way to end up at the end of a rope. We do something like that and we'd have not one but half a dozen posses after us."

"But they are themselves murderers—"

"Could be, but the law'd have only your word for that. Besides, Sandoval and Pacheco've got official papers showing they work for your government and giving them the authority to hunt you down."

"Those papers are false—"

"Must look pretty good. Somebody in the American army looked them over and assigned two soldiers to help them run us down. Now, you shoot them, and we'll really be in a pot of trouble."

"It is true," Bravo murmured. "This is not Mexico. We must remember."

"What then do we do?" Gomez asked impatiently. "Are we to run forever from these jackals who wish our lives? Can we not defend ourselves? Is there not forgiveness in your law for protecting one's own life?"

"Sure, but in a case like this—two agents of the Mexican government out to arrest the killers of a general—"

"Such was warranted—"

61

"Not saying it wasn't, but you can see how it looks and sounds to a lawman. He'd side with them."

Bravo gazed thoughtfully into the fire. "This matter of how your law would look upon us had not occurred to me. I see now how great your help will be needed. Without such we likely should find ourselves trapped, and hopeless."

Gomez drew out his cigarette makings, began to roll himself a cigarette. "Would such matter? There is little ahead for us in this life. As well we die as—"

"*No, companero*," Dominguez interrupted sternly, "there is much to live for. Once we have our gold and return to the Joaquin Valley, a new life will begin."

"How can you believe this?" Gomez demanded. "The friends of El Escorpion will never forget—"

"Such will be of no consequence. We shall have new names, and we have those in the valley who look up to us, who will help. And with gold all things can be made possible."

"Ah, the gold. First Amigo must be found and that in itself is a task of magnitude."

"Agreed, and since Shawn has pointed out the dangers and difficulties we face in a land of which we have so little understanding, I feel it would be wise to make better preparations."

"How so? He has provided us with food and has agreed to guide us to this village of Dodge City."

Starbuck smiled. The last time he had been in the

Kansas settlement it was far from being just a village.

"Yes, but as a kindness to us. Would it not be better to hire him for such purpose?"

"Hire me?" Starbuck echoed, coming to a sitting position. "What's the need? Said I'd get you to Dodge and I meant it."

"But if you were to receive payment—a hundred dollars gold from each of us, would you agree to take us to this place, aid us in finding and collecting our money from Amigo, and then seeing us safely returned to Mexico?"

"Yes, that is a good thought," Gomez declared. "You have spoken of looking for work. Would this not be a job of good pay?"

"Sure would—more than it'd be worth," Shawn agreed.

His plan had called for taking the vaqueros to Dodge City, helping them to find Amigo—hopefully, his missing brother—and parting from them at that point. He had given no thought to their return journey to the border. They would need help—and he could use the job, and most certainly that kind of pay! Three hundred dollars would carry him well into the next year. And if it turned out that Amigo was Ben—well, he'd handle the problem when he faced it.

"Is such agreeable, Shawn?" Bravo asked.

"Sure; like I say, I'm looking for a job and this one will suit me fine. . . . Wondering, though, about Ortega. He going to go for it?"

"Carlos will see the wisdom of such," Bravo assured him. "And if he does not, Francisco and I will bear his share of the cost."

"If he's against it you can forget his part—"

"There is small possibility of that," Gomez said dryly. "For Carlos to accept a favor from an *Americano* is to him unthinkable. He will pay and thus relieve his conscience."

Starbuck grinned. "Guess that settles that. Want you to know that this wasn't what I had in mind. Wasn't expecting to get paid for doing a favor, specially since I was heading that way."

"Yes, but it was not your plan to return."

"Well, no, had figured to find myself something to do around Dodge, or maybe go on up into Wyoming or the Dakotas."

"Therefore now such is unnecessary. You have found this job."

"That's it—and I reckon that puts a different slant on the whole business. If I'm to be responsible I'll want your word that you'll do what I tell you, and that I'll have full say on everything."

"Yes, of course—"

"Any of you striking out on your own could get us all in big trouble."

"It is understood."

"Means Ortega—particularly."

"Francisco and I will both talk with him," Bravo said. "He will agree to the necessity."

"That ought to help," Starbuck said, shrugging,

"but I've got a hunch it's going to take stronger measures on my part to make him see the light."

"Stronger measures? What is your meaning of that?"

"Let it ride," Starbuck murmured. "Time comes, you'll savvy."

Taking the corners of his woolen cover, he drew them about his body. A definite coolness was setting in and by morning it would be bitter cold. He glanced toward the rim of the butte. Ortega still maintained his vigil.

Gomez rose, blanket draped about him like a thick shawl. "I will talk to Carlos now," he said. "It is best we get it done."

Shawn lay back. "Be even better if you can talk him into getting some sleep, like I've mentioned. Goes for you—all of us. The Arena Blancas is a long ride from here."

"Arena Blancas?" Dominguez echoed. "In my language that means a place of white sand—"

"Just what it is—a big flat of sand so white that it can blind a man when the sun's full on it, if he's not careful. Once we're on the yonder side of it our chances for losing the posse are good. . . . See you in the morning."

"*Buenas noches*," Bravo replied, and settled back.

For a time Francisco remained motionless at the edge of the clearing, eyes on the dark, hunched figure of Ortega while he listened to the quiet

65

sounds of the night. And then, as if heeding a need to be utterly alone, he walked silently off toward a mound of rocks a short distance from the butte. Reaching it, he climbed to its low summit, and finding a flat boulder, sat down.

Before him, in the glittering night, spread the valley of the Rio Grande, a vast, gently rolling carpet. Its smoothness was broken here and there by dark patches of high brush and groves of trees. In the occasional places where the river cut back deeply into the land and became visible to him, it had a bright, silver sheen as it sped inexorably southward in its haste to reach Mexico.

Mexico. . . . He had a feeling that he had seen it for the last time, that never again would he ride through its green valleys, across its wide, breathless deserts, or climb its towering mountains. His time on earth was ending, and just as well for he had been no more than a living dead man since that hour when he had stood by and seen all who were dear to him slaughtered like animals in a pen.

Stricken, paralyzed, he had watched from the far side of a field as Jaramillo's soldiers did their grisly job, knowing that it was foolhardy, senseless, to try and stop them. Exposing himself would have meant death instantly—and uselessly.

Better that he had. To have raced out onto that open field and thus invited the bullets of the Scorpion's soldiers would have put an end to all then and there, and he could have died in peace with his loved ones. Fate had decreed otherwise, but for what purpose still remained obscure; he had accomplished nothing of value since that moment, and if he had been chosen by some power beyond and above men to participate in the salvation of his country, there had yet to come some indication of such.

True, he had been one of those to rid the world of Andres Jaramillo and a number of his officers and soldiers, but any man adept with knife and pistol could have accomplished that.

And now here he was in a foreign land, far from home, in company with Bravo Dominguez, who had visions of being a savior, Carlos Ortega, a man who believed in nothing, and a big, hard-jawed American named Shawn Starbuck, who seemed capable of all things. . . . Perhaps it was with them that he would discover the ultimate purpose for which he had been restrained from dying.

Far back in the short hills a wolf howled a lonely lament. Francisco stirred, got to his feet. We are brothers, you and I, he thought, alive by chance and marked for death. To what avail?

Desolate, he shrugged, looked toward the butte. Carlos had not stirred. He would wait, talk with him in the morning; he had not the spirit for argument now. Turning, he made his way down the mound and retraced his steps to the clearing.

10

They were mounted and on their way well before daylight the next morning, riding hard and fast for the nearby Organ Mountains. Starbuck was anxious to put the sprawling, ragged formation between his party and the posse as quickly as possible; and by the time the sun was breaking over the higher Sacramento Peaks farther to the east, they had passed through the Organs and were swinging north into the broad Tularosa Valley.

Shawn breathed easier at that point. There had been no signs of the posse and it would appear that Sandoval and Pacheco were continuing on up the Rio Grande Valley, following the trail they assumed the fugitives they sought had taken. Just how long it would take the Mexican agents to realize they had been tricked could only be guesswork, but Starbuck figured he and the vaqueros would gain at least a full day on them.

The crushing heat that filled the colorless rock bowl in which El Paso and its border counterpart, Juarez, lay, was behind them now, and in its stead a hot wind moved persistently across the land, lathering the horses and keeping the men bathed in sweat, but it was not too disagreeable.

"This is much like the Joaquin Valley where we lived," Bravo said as they pressed on steadily.

He was at Starbuck's left; a bit to their right, and

out of the dust kicked up by their horses, were Gomez and Carlos Ortega.

"Good cattle country," Shawn said, "but water's always a mite scarce. You have that trouble at home?"

Dominguez nodded slowly, abruptly remote and silent. After a long pause he murmured, "Home—it is but a place of memory now. There is nothing that remains except ruin."

"Still got the land."

"A house can be rebuilt, yes; but what it took my family generations to build—no. I grew up there, my father before me, his father before him. What they did can now be only something of remembrance. Do not Americans understand these things?"

"Sure, we understand them. We have tradition even if my country is just a couple of hundred or so years old, but I guess Americans are sort of restless. Most of them like to keep on the move, see what's on the other side of the next hill, and because of that they never get around to sinking any roots."

"But are there no great haciendas—plantations or farms where father has passed such on to son?"

"Not so much out in this part of the country, but in the South, and back East, there's plenty of places that have been in the same family for years. That'll start happening around here, I expect, when there're no more hills to climb and the land gets settled. . . . How'd Ortega take to your idea of hiring me for a guide?"

Bravo shrugged, smiled faintly. "As we had thought, he was not agreeable."

"Still won't trust me?"

"It is so, and I ask of you much patience for him."

Shawn glanced over his shoulder to their back trail. "Nobody tracking us—he can see that. What's it going to take to convince him?"

There was an edge of irritation to Starbuck's words. Many days and nights lay ahead during which they all would be thrown together closely, possibly in dangerous situations; having one of the party in a sullen, obstinate state of mind could only increase tension and heighten the chances for disaster.

Bravo shrugged. "It will come in time."

"That's not good enough. We maybe won't have the time."

Dominguez fell silent as they continued on. At mid-day they halted to rest themselves and the horses at the foot of a rocky outcropping where there was a small spread of shade afforded by a cluster of cedars.

Words were few, and as they sprawled on the heated sand, Starbuck felt Ortega's hard, dark eyes upon him. Temper short at best, he turned to the vaquero.

"If you've got something to say to me, get on with it!"

Carlos continued to stare for a long moment, turned his head and spat. "My words will come at the proper time," he said.

"Words about what?"

"That I am right in what I believe."

"And what's that?"

"No *Americano* can be trusted."

Shawn drew himself to a sitting position. "You still hanging on to the idea that I'm selling you out?"

Ortega met his angry glare calmly. "Yes—"

"How?" Starbuck demanded. "You don't see the Assassins on our trail, do you?"

"Perhaps they are not the ones who will pay you a generous reward."

Starbuck swore. "Use some sense! If I'd been after a reward we wouldn't be here—I would've brought that posse back with me when I went into Las Cruces, saved myself this long, hot ride."

"Possibly there was not an opportunity to do so. Also, you knew that I would be watching."

"I had the opportunity, all right, and I could have made use of it if—"

"It is best we travel on," Bravo cut in, rising. It was obvious he wished to end the tense conversation before it grew more bitter. "Is it far to this place of white sand, *compadre?*"

Shawn got to his feet slowly. "Be near dark by the time we can get there," he said indifferently. "Right now, before we pull out, I'd like to get a few things settled with Ortega."

"There is nothing to be settled, senor," Gomez said, coming into the conversation. "We have employed you to see us safely through this journey, and have put our faith and trust in you."

"Not Ortega, it seems," Starbuck said icily.

"We are two and he is one. Your promise to us is satisfactory—"

"*Palabra de gringo—nada!*" Ortega hissed, and turned toward the horses.

Shawn, rigid, jaw set, wheeled to Dominguez. "What's that mean?"

Bravo frowned. "Carlos says foolish things—"

"I have said that I do not trust the word of a gringo," Ortega answered defiantly.

Starbuck's temper flared. He took a step forward, halted as Bravo caught him firmly by the arm.

"As a favor, Shawn—"

"Sounds to me like I'm being called a liar!"

"No, it is different. He means he does not trust your promise to take us to Dodge City and back to Mexico. He feels that once you have been paid you will desert us."

"He's wrong again. Wasn't expecting to collect any pay until the job's done. That means when we're back in Mexico."

Bravo relayed the reply in quick Spanish to Ortega. The big vaquero listened, gave the words thought, made his comments, also in Spanish, and mounted his horse.

Dominguez nodded to Shawn. "It is understood."

"Maybe," Starbuck said, not moving. "Seems to me there was a lot more to what he said than that."

Bravo's shoulders stirred helplessly. "Only that he would have greater confidence if you were a Mexican such as us. He believes the word of a Mexican is more to be relied upon."

"Among our race there is honor between men," Ortega said, hands resting on the big horn of his heavy saddle. "Once the word is given it will never be broken."

"And you think no American ever keeps his promise?"

Ortega's mouth pulled down at the corners. "If such gringo exists, I have yet to meet him—"

"We have met him, Carlos!" Bravo cut in hastily. "Of this I am certain."

"Such is yet to be proved," Ortega said. "Truth burns clean. At that time we will know."

Anger smoldering within him, Starbuck turned away as the vaquero moved off, and swung onto his sorrel. It was impossible to reason with Carlos Ortega, and were it not for Bravo and Francisco, he wouldn't bother to try. But something had to give, he realized, casting a glance at their back trail to reassure himself that they were not being followed; he couldn't take many more of the vaquero's insults without doing something about it, regardless of the others.

11

"Pull up here!" Starbuck called back to the vaqueros.

The men had halted on a low mound a short distance away and were staring out across the vast expanse of bleached, white sand that unfurled before them like a snowy carpet. It was shortly before sunset and the gypsum particles were taking on a golden glint.

They had traveled hard and fast all that day in the wilting heat, and to pitch a camp on the weedy flat that he had selected was poor reward for their labors; but they were in country where nothing better was available unless they chose to double back to the San Andres mountains, a considerable distance to the west, where more suitable sites could be found. Since to do so would have taken them miles out of their way, Shawn had given it no thought.

Dismounting, he threw off his saddlebags and blanket roll, and was beginning to strip the sorrel when Bravo and the others rode in. Silent, they fell to similar chores, each man seeing to the care of his own horse before considering his own needs. The animals were picketed loosely in order to graze wide on the thin stand of grass, and watered sparingly from the dwindling supply in the canteens. Then Starbuck and the vaqueros set about preparing for the night.

"Best we build the fire in a hole," Shawn said as Gomez, hands filled with wood he had collected, looked questioningly at him. "Not so apt to be seen."

Francisco nodded, dropped to his knees, and began to scoop out a hollow in the loose soil. Nearby, Ortega, unbuckling the pockets of his saddlebags, paused to look back over the route they had traveled.

"The *Asesinos*, they—"

"Not them I'm thinking about," Starbuck replied, laying out food for the evening meal.

"Who then if not?"

"Apaches. Reservation's north of here. Now and then a bunch of braves will break out and go raiding for guns and horses. Always smart to be a little careful when you're in this part of the country."

The fire going, Gomez had set the two cans they now used for making coffee over the flames, after filling each with water. He tapped the canteen he was holding to indicate that it was near empty.

"There will be a place where this can be refilled tomorrow?"

Shawn nodded. "I remember a creek on ahead. Ought to reach it around noon. Can fill up there and water the horses—if it's not dry."

"And if it is dry?" Ortega asked, bristling.

"It then is dry," Bravo replied before Shawn

could answer. "It will not be the first time we have gone without water."

"Perhaps, but those were days when we had no choice," Ortega said. "With our gringo guide who is to be paid so well it would seem that such hardship could be avoided."

"He does not control the rain, the sun. It was a foolish thing to say."

Shawn, slicing potatoes into the spider where bacon was already sizzling, listened in tight-lipped silence. Ortega had filled the day with snide remarks. When it became apparent they had successfully shaken the Assassins and their posse, he found other things to comment on unfavorably, always managing somehow to throw blame upon Starbuck or cast aspersions on Americans in general.

"This is a place unfit even for goats," he said, glancing about. "Perhaps, had more thought been given to such we could have spent the night in the shelter of those mountains to the west. It would have been better for the horses as well as for ourselves."

Shawn paused, brushed at the sweat on his forehead with the back of a hand. Weary, nerves ragged from the hot wind that had plagued them since sunup, his temper was straining at its bounds.

"Idea was to put as much ground as possible between us and that posse, fast as we could, in case they were on our trail," he said in slow, distinct words. "Cutting straight across, not taking the good road that runs along the mountains, was the way to do it. . . . Now, if you want me to back off, let you handle—"

"Carlos!" Bravo broke in sharply. "It would be well to see to the horses!"

"No!" Ortega shouted. "It is better that I remain and say more of what is in my mind to this gringo who lies—"

Starbuck leaped to his feet as anger surged through him. In a half-dozen strides he crossed to where the vaquero stood. Ortega saw him coming, squared himself, a grin parting his lips and revealing his broad white teeth.

"Ha!" he said. "You would try—"

Starbuck's balled fist caught him solidly on the jaw, rocked him to one side, stilled whatever further words he intended to speak.

He caught himself, regained balance, and ducked low, then spun. A knife glittered in his hand. Shawn avoided a slashing sweep of the blade, kicked out, knocked the weapon from Ortega's grasp with a booted foot.

Carlos rasped something in Spanish, threw himself on Shawn. Momentum and weight drove Starbuck backward. He tripped, went down, with the vaquero on top, hammering at his head.

Linking his hands, Starbuck weathered the blows, drew back his arms their full length, and smashed his knotted fists into the Mexican's face.

Carlos grunted and blood spurted from his nose and crushed lips as he pulled back. Instantly Starbuck heaved his body, dislodged the man, and rolling away, bounded to his feet.

Ortega, agile as a cat despite his size, features smeared with blood, was after him instantly. Shawn continued to back away, allowing the vaquero to quicken his charge, and then abruptly halted. His left shot out, caught Ortega on the chin, turned the man half about. A short, vicious right to the jaw followed, and then a second left that landed on the ear.

Carlos staggered, arms falling to his sides. Shawn, fists cocked, beginning to suck for wind, circled the vaquero slowly, warily. Ortega drew himself up, shook his head as he sought to clear away the mist clouding his brain. From beyond the thin veil of dust stirred up by their scuffling feet, Bravo Dominguez and Gomez watched in silence.

Abruptly, Ortega recovered himself and charged. Shawn did not give way, met the lowered head of the vaquero with a sharp left and a hard right. As the man's movements stalled, he crowded in close, his arms now two relentlessly hammering pistons as he dealt punishment mercilessly, and then, untouched by the vaquero's awkwardly flailing fists, pivoted away.

Again he waited, allowed Ortega to carry the fight to him. When the Mexican bore in, he stepped nimbly aside, drove a solid, chopping right to the man's jaw. The vaquero wilted, arms once more dropping. Legs spread, eyes glazed, mouth open, he hung motionless. Shortly, he shook himself, drew on his reserve strength, mustered another charge.

Shawn, well schooled in the art of boxing by old Hiram, who could have been a ring champion had he not loved the land more, expertly avoided the clawing fingers that sought to seize him, bear him to earth. As the vaquero rushed in, he feinted, closed in, jabbing lefts and rights into the man's face until he halted, utterly helpless.

At that Starbuck turned away. Brushing at the sweat on his face, he picked up his hat, and returning to the fire, resumed his cooking duties. He was conscious of several aching pains where the vaquero's fists had found their target, but it was a good feeling and he had a sense of relief. Perhaps now Ortega would keep his uncalled-for remarks to himself.

Gomez had moved off to where the vaquero stood, hands at his sides, head down, black hair stringing over his battered features. Bravo touched Shawn lightly on the shoulder.

"It might have been wiser had you killed him," he murmured.

Starbuck looked up at the man. "No point in that. When you kill a man it has to be for a good reason. Having a loose mouth is not one."

"True, but Carlos is a proud man, and not one to

forget. His hate for *Americanos* will now be even greater."

Shawn drew himself erect. "I think you're making too much of this. Was only a fight—a way to get a few things settled. Now, I'll tell you the same as I did him, if you want me to pull out—"

"No, certainly not. It is that I wish to warn you to take care—"

"Starbuck—there is a campfire! By the mountains!"

The voice of Francisco Gomez cut into Bravo's words. Shawn wheeled, threw his glance toward the San Andres. A small red eye winked in the night.

"The *Asesinos!*" Bravo murmured in a falling tone.

"Maybe. Also could be Apaches or could be some pilgrim pulled up for the night. No way of telling from here."

Dominguez nodded. "Regardless, it is evident now why you did not wish to camp in the mountains. If the fire is that of the *Asesinos* they would have overtaken and captured us had we been there."

Shawn squatted, set the spider of stew off the fire, and picking up a twig, stirred down the froth in the cans of coffee.

"Learned a long time ago that a man better use his head if he expects to stay alive in this country. . . . Grub's all ready. Best we eat and turn in so's we can get another early start. That fire just might belong to Sandoval and Pacheco."

Ortega sat alone in the darkness nursing his aches and pains in silence. The big gringo Starbuck had fists like iron and the skill of a grenadier guard with a rapier when it came to using them. But it was not ended. He had been stupid, had been forced to fight the gringo's fight; it would not be so again.

He stirred wearily, looked out across the flats to the shadowy, irregular bulk of the distant mountains. The red spot of fire no longer shone in the night, and whoever it was camped close by had crawled into his sleeping blanket—or moved on. Could it be the Assassins? Most likely. They would never really get rid of Cruz Sandoval and his echo, Onofre Pacheco—not until both were dead, or they themselves were.

It would seem that he was wrong about Starbuck but he would reserve voicing such judgment until later on when there could be no doubt—and such would persist until they had completed their errand and were again in Mexico. Only then would he find it possible to make such an admission, for had not his father warned him against all Americans and had not his father always been right?

It was an American masquerading as a friend who had ruined his young sister; it was another one in whom there had been trust placed that stole his

mother and took her away for his own. All
Americans were not only capable of such deeds,
but were prone to committing them. Thus none
was to be trusted, and while Starbuck *seemed* to be
a man of honor, it was only prudent to wait and
see.

Regardless, there was now the matter of a personal score, one of honor, that had to be satisfied,
but that too must be delayed until a later date for
the sake of Bravo and the gold. When—and if—
the big gringo saw them safely through that project
to a conclusion, then he would have his hour. . . .
Meanwhile he would not relax his vigilance, or
decrease his suspicions. His father had never been
wrong; it was not likely he would be in this
instance.

Lying back, Carlos closed his eyes. He would
sleep now. Tomorrow was another day and he must
be ready to act should the American prove false.

12

"Indians!"

Starbuck hissed the warning to the men strung
out behind him on the trail, and instantly swerved
the sorrel in behind a clump of mesquite. Bravo,
Gomez, and last in the line, Carlos Ortega, his face
misshapen and discolored in many places, wheeled
in behind him.

It was late morning and they had pushed the

horses hard through the punishing heat without letup. There had been no indication of anyone following, and Starbuck would have liked to believe that the campfire at the foot of the mountains had not belonged to the Mexican agents and their soldier posse, but he was not accepting it as fact.

That their pursuers were not to be seen on the broad flat behind them was no proof they were not in the area; Sandoval and Pacheco and their party could be keeping to the west where they could ride unnoticed, planning to draw in close farther north where the country broke up into hills and forested slopes and they would not be noticed.

"Apaches?" Gomez asked, his eyes on the dozen or so riders moving out of a deep arroyo slashing directly across their course a short distance ahead.

Shawn studied the coppery figures. Naked except for breech cloth and a band tied around their head to keep the hair out of their eyes, they were dark, intent shapes in the streaming sunlight. A few had paint streaks on their faces.

"About have to be," he replied softly. "Kiowas and Comanches sometimes get this far west but this bunch looks more like Apaches."

"They are warlike?"

"Hostile? Never know for sure. Most of them are friendly now. Government put them on a reservation, place near here, right after the war ended, and they're supposed to stay there. But every now and then a few will break out and kick up trouble.

Unless you've got them outnumbered it's smart to steer clear of them."

"We have this trouble with the Yaquis, also with the Chiricahuas who raid the villages that are close to the border."

Shawn nodded grimly. He'd had a brush or two with the fierce Arizona branch of the Apache tribe himself.

"*Mira—mira!*"

Francisco Gomez spoke suddenly in Spanish, pointed. Bringing up the rear of the column were two men on foot. Their hands were bound behind them, and the ropes by which they were being led were drawn tight around their necks. Both were staggering, near exhaustion, but fearing death from strangulation, were fighting to stay on their feet.

"*Mexicanos!*" Ortega breathed in a harsh voice.

They were Mexicans, Shawn saw at that same moment. Likely the pair had been captured some time ago during a raid and were in the process of being traded. Gomez and Ortega moved forward. Starbuck raised his hand quickly.

"Careful! We start something, the first ones they'll kill will be the two prisoners."

"But we cannot permit them to make slaves of them," Francisco said in a low voice. "I will go alone if need be."

"Just sit tight—"

"That is all you will do?" Ortega demanded. "You will let them torture and kill our countrymen? Is it

84

because you fear there are many of them, only four of us? I do not turn back because of such."

Starbuck's jaw was a hard line. The odds were three, possibly four to one against them, and with the Assassins possibly somewhere in the near distance, they could ill afford any loss of time; but neither could they permit the Apaches to keep their prisoners.

Ignoring Ortega, he pointed to a rise in the land off to their left. The Indians were now dropping out of sight in the arroyo along which they were making their way.

"Apaches'll be passing below that bluff," he said, and spurring the sorrel out from behind the mesquite, quickly crossed the intervening ground.

Slipping from the saddle, he faced the vaqueros. Lifting his hand for quiet, he said, "Got to keep them from killing those two men. Means it'll be best to wait until the braves have ridden by and the prisoners are right below us. Then we'll open up."

Bravo and Gomez nodded their understanding. Ortega merely stared at him, a slight frown on his battered face.

Checking the horses to be certain they were securely tied to one of the several clumps of rabbitbush that dotted the slope, Starbuck drew his pistol. Then, crouched low, he led the way to the top of the butte. Short of the rim, he removed his hat, and dropping flat on his belly, wormed his way to the edge. The vaqueros moved in silently beside him.

Below, and a bit to the right, the braves were filing by, following the winding trace of the sandy arroyo. They appeared to be dozing; the odds were better, Starbuck thought, and started to pull back, outline a plan of attack now that they had the lay of the land.

A cry of pain broke the hush, the sound followed by guttural words in the Apache tongue. Shawn swung his attention to the source. One of the prisoners had fallen. His captor, ignoring the man's helplessness, was dragging him along the floor of the wash, giving him no opportunity to regain his footing.

"No!" Carlos Ortega shouted, jumping to his feet.

Starbuck tried to grab the vaquero, silence him before he betrayed their presence. He was too late. The Mexican was up and firing his pistol.

The Apaches wheeled in surprise, rushed to gain the cover afforded by the brush and rocks along the arroyo's sides as Shawn and the other two vaqueros began to add their fire to Ortega's. Three of the Indians went down. Carlos, now on one knee, steadied his weapon on a crooked arm and cut down a fourth as he raced to leave the arroyo which had become a trap for the braves.

Shawn, pistol empty, pulled back below the rim of the butte, hurriedly began to reload. The Apaches, recovering, were returning the shots.

Gomez flinched as one of their bullets grazed a forearm, left a bloody streak across his dark skin.

Abruptly the shooting ceased. Starbuck glanced up. The vaqueros, also having paused to reload, rose slowly, carefully. From below the bluff came the quick sound of horses racing off. Shawn moved to the rim.

The Apaches were leaving. Three lay dead in the sand immediately below, farther on was a fourth. Back close to the base of the butte were the two unfortunate prisoners.

"They have killed them," Gomez murmured at Shawn's elbow. "It was as you said it would be. . . . It would have been wise to wait, Carlos, as you were told."

Starbuck, not waiting to hear Ortega's reply, holstered his weapon, and followed by the vaqueros, dropped down into the wash. They were losing valuable time—critical, in fact, insofar as any lead they had on the Assassins was concerned, if indeed the Mexican agents and their soldiers were in the area. They would have heard the gunshots, and guessing that the men they sought were involved, would make haste to cover the miles that separated them.

But he said nothing about it, simply stood by quietly while the vaqueros cut the cords that bound their countrymen's hands, threw off the ropes looped about their necks, and then laid them, side by side, beneath a slight overhang in the face of the butte. Using sticks and their knives, they completed the burial by caving in the sandy soil upon the tortured bodies.

His theories concerning the Assassins could be unfounded, anyway; there was no good reason to believe that Sandoval and the others had turned back from the Rio Grande and were on their trail; it was only a possibility that he feared.

Regardless, there was no point in thinking about it now; what they had done had been necessary, for, as men, they were duty-bound to attempt a rescue of the prisoners the Apaches had taken. Starbuck's only regret was that Ortega had lost his head and had begun the attack too soon, thus voiding their chances of saving the two men.

But that, too, was now wind down the valley and nothing could be done to recall it. All they could do was push on.

13

The creek was low but, fortunately, not dry. They dammed up the lower end of a small pool, allowed it to deepen, and after filling their canteens, watered the horses.

It took the better part of an hour but there was no avoiding the loss of time; they were in a wide, desolate country where moisture in any form was at a premium, and to venture abroad without an ample supply was a serious, often fatal, mistake.

Camp that night was made at the edge of a volcanic lava bed that simmered with stored-up heat until long after the sun had gone down. Again Starbuck took care to conceal the small fire laid for cooking, and doused it immediately after the chore was finished. Later a careful search of the surrounding land was made from a high point in the black, cruel rock, but no signs of another camp were to be seen, a fact that cheered Bravo.

"It was not the *Asesinos*," he said, drawing his blanket about his shoulders to ward off the chill that, paradoxically, was setting in as the night aged.

"What I'm hoping," Shawn replied.

He would like to believe it now just as he would have earlier, but always a cautious man at such times, he could not be sure, could not chance relaxing his vigilance. It was only natural to believe that the Mexican agents, if they were nearby, would be taking the same care as they to conceal their presence. It was far better to assume that to be the fact than be caught unawares.

They rode out early that next morning, the day's destination being an ancient Indian ruins that would offer more comfortable camping facilities. It could even be a good thought to lay over there for a day or so if there was still no indication of pursuit, Starbuck decided. They had pushed the horses hard from the moment they had left El Paso, and all were in need of rest.

By noon they had pulled out of the lava flats onto a high prairie. Mountains of size were visible to the north and the heat had decreased. Traveling should be less arduous once they left the semi-desert and were within the forested hills, Shawn thought—but it was still a long way to Dodge City.

Dodge City. . . . Would he find Ben there? Was he the Amigo the vaqueros had been in league with? Could the search be coming to an end—or was he to meet disappointment once again as he had in the past? Failure had occurred so many times now that it no longer cut deep and lowered his spirits to the point of depression. He stolidly accepted disappointment much as one tolerated the heat and cold of the changing seasons.

"This Amigo," he said, turning to Bravo, riding on his left as the horses plodded abreast up a long grade spotted with patches of golden mallow, "what kind of a man is he?"

Ortega, on the far side of Gomez to Shawn's right, leaned forward, rested a forearm on the big horn of his heavy Mexican saddle. He had kept pretty much to himself since the fight.

"Why do you ask again? There perhaps is reason for so much interest in him?"

Starbuck grinned. Things were back to normal; Carlos Ortega was his same bellicose, suspicious self.

"Could be," he murmured.

He could tell them, he supposed, of the possibility that Amigo was the brother for whom he was searching, but once more dismissed the thought in the belief that it could serve no good purpose. Revealing his interest could, in fact, heighten Ortega's skepticism and create more problems, and that he could do without. Later, when the moment was right, he'd make his explanations.

"Is it possible you have acquaintance with this Amigo?" Ortega pressed.

"Know a lot of people. Been knocking around the country for quite a spell. Could be somebody I've met," Starbuck replied, and turned his attention back to Bravo. "You never answered my question."

Dominguez shrugged. "There was not the opportunity," he said, nodding slightly at Ortega. "But he was a man much like yourself, not so tall but with dark hair and light eyes."

"Were they blue?"

The vaquero gave that thought, shook his head. "Of that I cannot recall. He laughed much, enjoyed the fighting and the danger."

It could be Ben, from what little he knew of him, which was practically all hearsay and secondhand. His brother's eyes, however, were definitely blue, like those of their father. There was also a scar that could serve as a positive identification, but since it was almost hidden by the left eyebrow it was visible only upon close examination.

He wished now, as he had many times in the

91

past, that he could furnish an accurate description of Ben when making inquiries, but it was not possible and such had contributed to the difficulty of the quest.

Movement to his left cut into Starbuck's thoughts. Hand dropping instinctively to the pistol on his hip, he swung his attention to that point. He relaxed. It was only an aged shepherd tending a small herd of goats in a grassy hollow.

The old man rose from the blanket upon which he was sitting, called to the dog that rushed forward barking furiously, brought him to a stop. Gomez raised a hand in greeting.

"Como esta, viejo?"

"Bien, bien. Usted?"

"They are exchanging greetings," Bravo translated to Shawn. He listened to the continuing flow of Spanish. "It is about the goats. They fare well but the grass grows poor in this valley and soon he will be taking them to the mountains where it is better."

"Ask him if he's seen any other travelers."

Dominguez relayed the words. The old man wagged his head, voiced a question of his own.

"He says no one has passed this way in the last days and asks if we have seen any Indians. Ortega is telling him of the party we encountered, and of their prisoners."

Shawn listened to the account, unintelligible to him, and throughout which the goat herder continually shook his head. When Carlos had finished he had words of his own.

"The old one says he has heard of the two men the Apaches had captured. They were prisoners for many days and suffered much. It is good they are dead, he says, for they would have not lived to see Mexico again. He wishes he could return to the village of his birth in Mexico. Everything is peaceful there."

"Probably not as peaceful as he thinks," Shawn observed, throwing a glance over his shoulder.

"Doubtless he has not heard of the change," Bravo agreed.

There were no riders to be seen, but the rolling contour of the land, broken by many arroyos, clumps of brush, and small groves of cedars, afforded ample cover for anyone wishing not to be seen.

"Ask him how far it is to the old Indian ruins," Shawn directed.

Bravo voiced the question. The old shepherd ran a gnarled hand through his thin, gray hair, gestured toward the north, and spoke briefly.

"A few hours by horse, he says. We will reach there before sundown."

Starbuck nodded. "About what I figured, but we'll have to move along to make it. Best tell him that if anyone comes along asking if he's seen us, he'll be doing us a favor by telling them nothing."

Ortega took it upon himself to state the request,

evidently going into considerable detail on the matter. When he finished, the old man bowed slightly and raised his hand in a farewell.

Carlos and the others responded, murmuring *Adios* as they rode by.

"Been better if we hadn't run into him," Starbuck said, touching the brim of his hat with a forefinger. "As soon nobody would see us."

"There is no need for worry," Ortega replied. "The old one is a man of honor. I explained to him about the *Asesinos*. He will tell them nothing if asked—not even if tortured. To him, as with all our kind, to give one's word is a matter of sacred trust."

Starbuck did not rise to the bait, merely smiled as they moved on.

The sun was gone when they reached the ruins, a large, sprawling mass of crumbling, gray rock walls, collapsed huts, and mounds of rubble. Shawn led the way to an area at the north end. He had once camped there with a party of cowhands riding to Texas where jobs as trail hands awaited them.

"Plenty of wood there," he explained, "and the walls are high enough to cut off the wind if it gets to blowing."

"There is water also?"

"Nope, big reason why the Indians pulled stakes when they did, I expect. Have to make do with what we've got until tomorrow. Be able to fill up then."

"There is plenty in the canteens," Gomez said.

They reached the section of the ruin recalled by Starbuck, halted, and set up their camp. Later, after the meal was over and they sat about enjoying the coolness, Shawn mentioned the advisability of laying over a day to rest the horses. All agreed it was a good idea, and shortly, with Ortega taking up his customary sentry post, they turned in for the night.

They rose later than usual the next morning, went leisurely about the business of preparing a meal. When it was finished they would see to the well-being of the horses, rubbing them down, checking and cleaning hooves, and doing whatever else was needed.

The hours ahead thus planned, they helped themselves to their portions of the food and settled back to enjoy it. Abruptly gunshots ripped through the hush.

As one they leaped to their feet, lunged for the protection of a nearby wall. A dozen bullets dug into the hard, dry soil, sent up spurts of powdery dust; one clanged against the iron spider, screamed off into space.

Crouched low, Starbuck peered over the rocks, seeking the location of the bushwhackers while he wondered grimly who they might be. Indians? Outlaws? Or could it be the posse?

Bravo voiced the answer to the question in the next moment, when a man in the bright red and blue uniform of the Mexican army moved cautiously into view at the far end of the ruins.

"The *Asesinos*!" he said tensely. "They have found us."

14

Starbuck, taut, angry with himself for his lapse of precaution, worked his way to the end of the wall. He wasn't certain if the men of the posse were together in one position or had been deployed.

Behind him, in the pall of dust raised by the persistent bullets, he could hear Bravo Dominguez' voice, low and angry, speaking of the *viejo*—the old man. Evidently he was blaming the herder for revealing their whereabouts, the truth of which was only too evident; anyone seeking them would have had to be told where they planned to camp. But they shouldn't condemn the shepherd too severely; more than likely the Assassins forced him to talk.

Lead smashed into the wall above Shawn's head, sprayed him with age-old dust. Flinching, he drew back. But he had his answer; the posse had separated, undoubtedly were still moving about in the hopes of improving their positions. Twisting around, he faced Bravo and the others.

"They've got us pinned down. We try to get to the horses, they'll pick us off like sitting ducks—

but if we stay put, they'll finish circling until they'll get us in a crossfire."

Ortega, a dark scowl on his features, was staring at the distant wall behind which the posse was hiding. He spat out a stream of Spanish, checked the pistol in his hand to be certain it was fully loaded.

"I will charge them," he said then, in English. "When they bring their guns to bear on me, you will run to the horses."

"Forget it," Starbuck said, studying the maze of offset, broken walls rising between them and the Assassins. At one time they had been the partitions between rooms in the fortlike arrangement. "I think we can work our way out of this without anybody getting hurt."

At once Bravo was at his side. "How, senor? If we fall back we become targets—"

"Don't figure to fall back," Shawn said, pointing to a wall a dozen steps in front of them. Half gone, it was still some four feet or so in height. "We move toward that, they can't see us."

"But to what advantage?"

"Once we reach that wall, we can follow along it to the next one."

"Will that not take us nearer to their guns?"

"For a ways, but we can keep moving to the left until we get to the main part of the ruin. Once there we ought to be able to double back to the horses without being seen."

"I will not flee those jackals," Ortega declared. "Better to face them like men—"

"That, too, is my thought," Gomez said. "I do not choose to run farther."

"This is not in the nature of running, as would a coward," Bravo said, frowning. "It is getting oneself out of a trap where death awaits—much the same as a wolf caught in a rope snare. There is no disgrace in escape."

Ortega nodded slowly. "Yes, better to leave and thus be able to fight again one day on equal terms. You are right, Bravo."

"I will stay," Gomez said flatly.

"Nobody stays!" Starbuck snapped. "You hired me to get you to Dodge City and I aim to do it."

At the harsh words Francisco turned to Shawn, smiled faintly. "*Si, senor*," he murmured.

"All right, let's get out of here," Starbuck said, turning to Bravo. "Want you going first. When I say the word, make a run for that wall. When you get there, wait. Understand?"

Dominguez said, "I do," and crouched.

Shawn made a swift survey of the surrounding rocks and rubble, saw no sign of the posse members or the betraying glint of sunlight on a rifle or pistol barrel.

"Now—"

Bravo leaped to his feet, raced across the narrow strip of open ground. No bullets challenged him. Either the move had taken the Assassins and their soldiers by surprise or they were not being watched as closely as he had anticipated. He glanced about. Ortega was hunched beside him, ready to take his turn.

"Go," he said.

Carlos rose, legged it for the wall. Rifles crackled. Bullets thudded into the hard soil, dogged his heels, but he made it safely.

Shawn leveled his pistol at the distant rim of weathered rock where puffs of smoke had revealed the location of a rifle.

"I'll cover you," he said to Francisco. "When I start shooting, move out."

"As you wish," Gomez replied. "But who will be here to cover, as you call it, you?"

"I'll manage. Ready?"

"I am."

Starbuck, holding his pistol with both hands, leveled it at the noted point on the wall. "Go," he said, and began triggering the weapon.

Gomez leaped to his feet, rushed toward his waiting companions. Only one gun disputed his passage, the other efficiently blocked by Shawn's accurately placed shots.

Settling back, Starbuck punched out the spent cartridges in the cylinder of his weapon, reloaded, and moved into place. The vaqueros were waiting for him, had their pistols out.

"Come!" Bravo shouted.

At the word all three began to fire, guns held

above their heads and aimed in the general direction of the posse. Starbuck, hunched low, made the dash across with only a scatter of shots being thrown at him.

In the haze of dust and powder smoke now drifting about, Shawn led the way to the adjoining room, and then, slipping through a gap in its opposite wall, crossed to the next.

One by one, on hands and knees, they continued working their way through the maze until they broke out into a large room. It apparently was a meeting place, or perhaps the site for ceremonials, Starbuck guessed. He moved toward a back corner where a break in the stacked rocks offered an exit. Passing through the opening, they found themselves in a sort of corridor that ran north and south, likely one that would take them to the room in which they had left their horses and gear.

"Think this is what we're looking for," Starbuck said, resting against the cool surface of the wall. Every muscle in his body was complaining at the unusual strain being placed upon it. "Ought to take us to where we can grab our stuff and pull out of here."

Bravo nodded. "I can smell the horses. . . . Would it not be best if one of us waited behind to keep watch while the rest prepared for riding?"

It was a good idea, Shawn agreed. "They could be trying to slip up on us."

"It is a task for me," Gomez said instantly before anyone else could volunteer.

Ortega protested, claiming it was his right, but Francisco waved him off, and Starbuck, with Bravo and Carlos close on his heels, hurriedly crawled along the base of the wall of the corridor and gained the room beyond. He muttered in satisfaction. He'd guessed right; the horses were there.

Entering quickly, they hastily saddled the mounts and collected their gear, being careful not to expose themselves to the men stationed behind the lower wall. Fortunately most of the cooking equipment had already been put away when the attack began, and they would lose only the cans used for cups and their improvised plates, which they had dropped when the Assassins opened fire on them in the adjoining room.

Shawn, the reins of his sorrel in his hand, gear packed, turned to Bravo and Ortega. They were ready also, had the black that Gomez rode in tow.

"We cannot return for Francisco—"

"No," Starbuck said in reply to Bravo's half question. "We'll lead the horses straight on. That'll take us out of the ruins at the upper end. I'll signal Gomez, have him drop back, meet us there. You go ahead."

Bravo reached for the sorrel's leathers, and the two vaqueros moved out, leading the horses along a narrow passageway that at times scraped the stirrups of the saddles. Shawn, again keeping low, returned to the room where he had last seen Gomez. The Mexican was not in sight. Swearing impatiently, Starbuck hurried along the wall. They didn't have much time left if Sandoval and Pacheco had plans to close in from the sides. Such could be underway at that very moment.

He saw Francisco a moment later, beckoned to him to fall back. Gomez complied immediately, and together they backtracked to the end of the passageway where Carlos and Bravo waited with the horses. A dozen strides beyond them a tumbled wall indicated the extreme north end of the ruins.

"You see any of them?" Shawn asked of Gomez as they went to the saddle.

"No one," Francisco answered. "It was as if they had gone."

"That can only mean they're trying to circle, get in behind us," Starbuck said tightly as he swung the sorrel about and spurred for the break in the line of rocks.

Instantly guns opened up on them from three sides. Shawn felt a bullet pluck at his arm, twisted about, fired point-blank at one of the Mexican soldiers appearing suddenly at the end of a wall. The man staggered, fell, his rifle clattering noisily into the rubble.

Guns were hammering steadily as the vaqueros returned the fire, and dust and smoke swirled in the narrow corridor.

"Keep moving!" Shawn yelled. "Get out in the open!"

They were caught in a merciless crossfire, and while the slope beyond the ruins offered little in the way of solid protection, it would be better than where they were.

He roweled the nervous sorrel toward the edge of the rocks. Through the dense haze he could see the shadowy shapes of two riders—Ortega and Bravo, he thought, but he could not be sure. It could be Francisco Gomez instead of Dominguez.

Suddenly he was in the clear, the big gelding stepping high to get through the welter of scattered rocks. Ahead he saw Carlos, and then Bravo. They had paused, were shooting toward the ruins, but their bullets were aimed high—at the top of the nearest wall—in order to hit neither him nor Francisco.

Francisco broke out of the smoke and dust. He was leaning far to one side and his streaked face showed pain. Immediately behind him a Mexican soldier appeared, and then one of the Americans.

"Francisco—behind you!" Shawn yelled, and snapped a shot at the nearest of the two.

Gomez swung his horse about, coolly raised his pistol and fired at the two soldiers, who were both leveling rifles at him. The reports came as one. The blue-uniformed cavalryman rocked backward, went down. Gomez sagged on his saddle, struggled to an upright position, aimed his weapon at the Mexican soldier. Beyond them the remainder of the posse began to appear, all firing as they came.

Shawn, triggering his weapon as fast as he could, rode in toward Gomez. "Francisco—come on!"

Gomez half turned. A half smile was on his lips. He dropped the black's reins, made a feeble gesture with the hand, continued to work his pistol with the other. A solid burst of gunfire came from the posse. Gomez buckled, fell from his horse.

Starbuck wheeled, raced to overtake Bravo and Ortega, riding hard for a grove of pines a quarter mile in the distance. They heard him coming, slowed.

"Francisco?" Bravo asked in a strained voice as he drew abreast.

"Dead," Shawn replied. "Was him that held them back so's we could get clear. Keep riding! Be wrong to throw away what he gave his life for."

15

Hunched low on their saddles, stirrup to stirrup, they pounded across the flat for the pine-studded slope. Rifles continued to crackle from the edge of the ruins. Bullets spurted sand ahead and behind them, and once Starbuck felt the tug of one tearing through a sleeve. Then, finally, they gained the protection of the trees.

Pulling the winded sorrel to a halt, Shawn swung

about. Bravo and Ortega, faces grim, wheeled in beside him.

"Francisco—he died brave?" Ortega asked in his stilted way.

Shawn nodded somberly. "If it hadn't been for him we'd still be back there."

A few moments of silence followed Starbuck's reply and then Bravo said: "With him it could be no other way. He was in love with death, that man. . . . What of the posse?"

"Think we got a couple of them, not sure."

"Sandoval or Pacheco?"

"Neither one—was a couple of the soldiers that I saw go down."

Ortega muttered in Spanish. "It would be so. They have charmed luck. No bullet can touch them, only those who ride with them."

Shawn rode forward a short distance, looked across the long, gently flowing land to the ruins. The dust and smoke had almost cleared away, and now the broken, sagging walls appeared forsaken. High above, two vultures had appeared, were gliding in wide, effortless circles, their soaring shapes etched blackly against the blue sky.

"Guess they were behind us all the way," Starbuck said. "Didn't fool them back at Las Cruces much as I'd hoped. . . . Best we move out. Won't take them but a few minutes to get their horses and follow."

"Let them," Ortega said, his dark eyes on the distant, irregular sprawl of gray rock. "Again I say it is time for an accounting."

"No," Dominguez cut in before Shawn could voice opposition. "In this country we cannot fight them. This is not Mexico."

"They have killed Francisco—"

"True, but it was in the name of the law as Shawn has explained to us. I have tried to make you understand."

"The law is wrong! What law is it they represent?"

"Of Mexico. I agree that is not wholly true, but in the eyes of the American lawmen they are officials and are accepted as legal representatives of our country."

"And you can figure on it being tougher for us from now on," Starbuck said. "Pacheco and Sandoval will report the shooting just as soon as they can get to a sheriff or marshal. They'll say we shot down two soldiers in the performance of their duty, and ask for more help in tracking us. Probably get out murder warrants."

"And poor Francisco—"

"They'll say he was killed resisting arrest."

Ortega fell silent. Bravo lowered his head. "I wish only that we could bury him. It is not likely the *Asesinos* will trouble to do so."

Starbuck pulled the gelding about, studied the towering hills to their left. Beyond them, in the west, lay the Rio Grande Valley with the river cut-

106

ting its wide path down the center. To follow along the east side of the mountains would be to reach Santa Fe by a different route—a natural course.

The two Mexican agents would be thinking of that also and the odds were good that, failing in their efforts to effect a capture of their fugitives, they would continue the pursuit to the old Spanish capital, convinced their quarry would have gone there.

The smart thing to do was avoid Santa Fe, angle more to the east, with Las Vegas as their destination. From there they could intersect the old Santa Fe Trail Cutoff, follow it on a more or less direct line for Dodge City.

It might throw the posse off their heels, give them a little breathing space—and it possibly would not fool the Mexicans at all. He'd thought he'd sent them up the Rio Grande Valley on a feather-in-the-wind chase, but instead they had outguessed him and swung east through the Organ Mountains, too. Regardless of what the vaqueros thought of the pair, they were not fools.

Touching the sorrel with his spurs, he came about, headed deeper into the pines. The trick he'd tried at Las Cruces was worth attempting again— and this time it just might work. When they reached the next town he'd put it into effect.

The settlement was called San Antonito, a small village nestled in a narrow valley at the foot of the mountains. Consisting of no more than a dozen houses, each with its plot of farmed land, it did boast a church, a general store, and a saloon.

Halting at the edge of the one street that wound through it, Starbuck gave the surrounding country his careful consideration. Pinon, juniper, and pine trees covered the steep slopes that lifted from either side, and higher up, beyond the oak brush and mountain mahogany, he could see stands of ghostly, white aspen, their leaves trembling in the light breeze.

"Is it not foolish to let ourselves be seen here?" Bravo wondered. "The *Asesinos* will pass this way, ask of us."

Starbuck nodded. "What I want them to do, only this time we'll make it plainer than we did in Las Cruces."

"How is that, senor?"

"I'll explain as we go along," Shawn said, and put the sorrel into motion.

With Ortega on one side, Bravo Dominguez on the other, he rode slowly down the lane, deep with shadows now as the sun dropped lower beyond the crags and ridges to the west. A half a dozen men loafed in front of the saloon, and the town marshal, a graying oldster who appeared suddenly in the doorway of his office with a shotgun cradled in his arms, eyed them warily as they passed.

Starbuck nodded to him. "This the road to Santa Fe?"

108

The lawman's expression did not change. "Reckon it is."

Starbuck said, "Obliged," touched the brim of his hat with a forefinger, and swung his attention forward again.

It could not have worked out better. What few persons in San Antonito who did not actually see them would hear of the three strangers who passed through the village asking of the way to Santa Fe. Sandoval and his partner Pacheco would have no difficulty in ascertaining that they had indeed been following that route and were heading for the capital.

Shawn glanced back. A bend in the road cut off all view of the settlement. Turning his attention to the slope to their right, he immediately veered off into a shoulder-high stand of crownbeard flourishing in a rain-water sink and started the climb toward a rocky shelf a quarter mile or so above the valley's floor.

"*Por que?*"

Shawn heard Carlos Ortega voice his question plaintively to Bravo. Without looking back, he said, "We'll be camping up here for the night."

There followed a time of silence during which only the squeak of saddle leather and the thump of horses' hooves could be heard, and then Bravo broke the quiet.

"I comprehend! It was for purpose that we were seen in the village and that the lawman was asked about the way to Santa Fe."

"Same as at Las Cruces—only a little plainer. Makes me jumpy to have that posse dogging our heels, and since this is the only road through here that ends up in Santa Fe, I don't figure they'll get suspicious and double back—leastwise not before morning."

"They are close—"

"Another reason why I want to get behind them. We run into some bad luck, they could be on us before we got a chance to pull out of sight."

"It is a good plan," Bravo said. "Believing themselves to be near, it is possible they will continue to ride through the night in hope of overtaking us. Do you not think so?"

"Sure do. They'll never be certain we're not in front of them, and by daylight it'll be too late to do anything about it."

"They will lie in ambush at the edge of Santa Fe when this becomes apparent," Ortega said. "How will we avoid this if there is but one road entering?"

"Not going to Santa Fe," Shawn answered as he veered the sorrel to right angles and moved toward a narrow clearing back off the rock shelf.

"Why is this?" Bravo asked in surprise.

"It'll be smarter to head out cross-country for Las Vegas. Save a lot of miles and maybe we can lose Sandoval and Pacheco for good."

"They pass now—" Ortega warned suddenly.

Starbuck drew to a quick stop. The posse had

been nearer than he'd expected. They had undoubtedly pushed their horses hard to make up time. A few minutes earlier and they would have seen him and the vaqueros leaving the road.

"Keep behind the brush," he cautioned.

Five riders. . . . The two agents, one Mexican soldier, his uniform still bright, and the two American cavalrymen, one of whom was wounded. They were moving at a lope, hopeful, no doubt, of spotting the fugitives they pursued before darkness set in.

"The trick has worked," Bravo said with a sigh as the posse disappeared around a bend in the winding road. "It is good not to have them at our backs."

"It is much better than good," Ortega added, his eyes on the point where the riders were last seen. Reaching for his peaked hat, he held it aloft in mock farewell. "*Adios, hombres*," he murmured. "May the road be rough and your saddles hard."

16

Despite the absence of a creek or spring anywhere nearby on the slope, the clearing back of the ledge made for a good camp. Wood was plentiful for a small, carefully placed fire, and pine needles in abundance provided them with their first comfortable bed in some time.

"This town of Las Vegas," Bravo said late that

evening as they sprawled on their blankets close to the low flames, "is it far from Dodge City?"

Starbuck spent a moment in calculation. "Probably take us a week, maybe a little less to make the ride."

Reaching out for a handful of dry branches, he tossed them into the wavering flames. At that altitude a chill had set in early, almost with sundown.

"So long a journey," Bravo murmured wearily.

"And for nothing, perhaps," Ortega added.

Starbuck shrugged. "Not many guarantees in this life."

"Only that one day a man dies," Ortega said.

Off in the direction of San Antonito a gunshot sounded, the echoes bouncing back and forth between the walls of the narrow valley in a series of diminishing reports.

"That cantina," Dominguez said, thinking back to when they had passed through, "it would be good to have a drink of tequila—or of your whiskey. It has been many days since."

"Can't risk it," Shawn replied, listening absently to the racket several dogs in the village, disturbed by the lone gunshot, were setting up. "Can be sure the marshal there's been told all about us and what we're wanted for."

We. . . . He mulled over the plural pronoun in his mind. It was the vaqueros, not him, the Mexican agents wanted—at least that was the way of it in the beginning, before he'd dealt himself into the game.

He had not known at that time what the true situation was when he'd taken sides with Bravo Dominguez there in the Longhorn Saloon, had reacted simply because he didn't like the odds and the way matters were shaping up for the vaquero. From then on each step he'd taken had put him deeper into the entanglement until now he was a wanted man, hiding on a mountainside, in company with acknowledged killers. Whether they were justified in what they and their partners had done was something a judge and jury must determine, but the fact remained that he was now a part of it, and with them was dodging the law.

Like as not Sandoval and Pacheco, to bolster their case, were telling that he was the American involved in the murder of Andres Jaramillo, the Scorpion, and therefore entitled to no more consideration than Bravo Dominguez and Carlos Ortega.

Starbuck shifted his position, turned his warmed side from the fire to favor the opposite, now feeling the bite of cold. . . . Well, what was done was done. He'd gotten himself into it, and he reckoned he'd be able to get himself out. It certainly wasn't the first time in his search for Ben that he'd found himself in a tight spot.

It was, however, one of the few times, if not the only occasion, he had ended up on the opposite side of the law, he realized, and that gave him an uncomfortable feeling. Right or wrong, the two Mexican agents were carrying papers and credentials that gave them the authority to act for the Mexican law officials, and because of such, their position would be respected and cooperation would be extended to them by lawmen in the territories and states through which they passed.

Accordingly, it was useless to expect any help from any sheriff or marshal they encountered. Such men would be bound by oath to aid the Mexicans in effecting a capture, unless— Starbuck's thoughts came to a halt. . . . Unless he could get to one with whom he was acquainted and outline the entire incident, from the crushing of the village in the Joaquin Valley by the Scorpion to the present moment; and who better to make such an explanation to than the lawman in Dodge City where they were headed—Wyatt Earp.

He'd met the man some time back, liked him, knew him to be fair and honest. Earp had been a deputy marshal then, probably now had been elevated to chief of the town's law force. Once he knew the details, Shawn was certain the case against Bravo and Carlos, as well as his own involvement, could be cleared up. Naturally, Wyatt Earp was not one to countenance murder, but he would listen to the facts and be willing to investigate the authenticity of Sandoval and Pacheco's status.

The dogs had ceased their barking, and back in the high ridges a cougar screeched as he prowled in the bright moonlight. The fire had dwindled to a mere glow and both vaqueros were asleep. In the morning he'd tell them of his plan to talk with Earp.

The sharp, early morning cold got them up long before sunrise. Silent, they went about the necessary chores each had assumed—preparing the meal, saddling the horses, getting the gear ready for loading, and such. Once the food was eaten, washed down by steaming, black coffee, all began to loosen up, become more cheerful.

Carlos—his attitude toward Starbuck much improved since the incident with the Apaches and the encounter with the posse at the ruins—drained the last of his coffee from the tin he used as a cup, motioned toward the north.

"The *Asesinos*, they will be in Santa Fe by this hour?"

"Would've been a hard ride. More than likely, they're somewhere this side and are figuring to get there around the middle of the morning—all depending on whether they pulled up for the night."

"But they will be far ahead of us and on a different road?" Bravo asked.

Shawn nodded. "Truth is, we'll be cutting cross-country. Be no road, only game trails, or none at all."

"Ah, that is good. . . . What of the canteens? All are near empty."

Starbuck finished his coffee. "Spring Canyon's

on up the valley a piece. Can fill them and water the horses there, then line out for Las Vegas."

Ortega let his glance travel over the towering, wild-looking land to the north and east. "It is country that extends no welcome—"

"Can't deny that, but either we cut across or take the road to Santa Fe. We've got just two choices."

"It is not being questioned, senor," Carlos said apologetically. "I merely make note of the difficulty."

A short time later they were again on the move, keeping to the regular route, as was necessary, until they reached the trail that swung off and led to the canyon where water was to be found. The path was well marked and showed considerable use, thus no difficulty was presented, and mid-morning found them halting beside the stream, a short, rushing strip of icy water that gushed from beneath a ledge of granite, exposed itself for a hundred yards or so, and then disappeared again into the gray rocks.

Shawn, slightly ahead of the others, held the anxious sorrel in check, a vague uneasiness troubling him. He could see no one, and the hoof prints visible here and there in the open ground appeared to be old. After a moment he shrugged, dismounted; he was getting jumpy as a buck deer. Dominguez and Ortega moved in beside him, swung off their saddles, allowed their horses to crowd in next to the sorrel.

"Just stand easy, gents."

Starbuck swore deeply as a voice reached out to them from the brush on the opposite side of the stream. His hunch had been right; there had been someone lurking in ambush—several men, in fact, he realized as he watched half a dozen figures step into view.

"What the hell's this all about?" he demanded, venting his anger. The men had drawn their pistols, had them leveled at him and the vaqueros.

The leader of the party, a step or so in front of the others, sighed heavily, lowered his weapon. The upper tips of a star peeked out from his shirt pocket.

"It's all right, boys," he said. "It ain't him."

A lawman with a posse, Starbuck realized. He threw a quick glance at Bravo and Ortega, shook his head slightly, and all waited silently while the riders holstered their pistols and shuffled nearer to the stream. Several bent at once, scooped up handfuls of water, and slaked their thirst eagerly.

"Didn't aim to give you all a start," the lawman said. "Name's Belden—deputy sheriff of this county. We figured you for an outlaw and a couple of his pals that we've been on the lookout for. Jasper they call Billy the Kid. Supposed to be somewhere between here and Santa Fe. You come up from the south?"

Ortega had dropped to his haunches, was conversing with one of the posse members, a young

Mexican. Bravo was collecting the canteens preparatory to filling them.

Starbuck nodded. "From the south—San Antonito."

That Pacheco and Sandoval had not run into Belden and his men was evident, otherwise the deputy would be making his arrests at that moment.

"You see anybody on the road? The Kid's young-looking and he'd a had three or four others with him."

"Sure didn't."

The lawman nodded, pulled a cigar from his shirt pocket, and thrust it between his teeth. "Yeah, expect he's farther up the line. Word I got on him was a mite old. Probably was twenty miles farther on by the time it come to me. . . . You camping here?"

Shawn glanced around, tension no longer gripping him tight. "Be a good spot," he agreed.

"Won't find one much better," Belden said, and turned his attention to his men. "If you're done watering, boys, let's move out. The Kid's some-wheres 'tween us and Santa Fe, I reckon, and if we put the iron to them nags we're forking, we might overhaul him."

The posse pulled back into the dense stand of dogwood, wild cherry, and other growth that lined the stream. Belden paused long enough to satisfy his thirst. Then they all disappeared. Moments later the sounds of their going faded. Starbuck glanced at Bravo. The vaquero had filled the canteens, returned them to the saddles. The horses had satisfied their needs, were now nibbling at the short grass.

"Let's get out of here," he said, turning to the sorrel. "We want to be long gone if that posse runs into Sandoval and Pacheco, and they start talking."

The vaqueros went onto their saddles at once, swung in behind Starbuck, now guiding his mount onto a faint trail that bore directly away from the stream. For a good quarter hour they rode steadily, working deeper into the pines and other evergreens. After breaking out finally into a lengthy, narrow valley, Shawn slowed the pace. Behind him he heard Ortega speak.

"*El Chavito—muy macho!*" he said, and continued on in Spanish.

Starbuck waited until he had finished, glanced inquiringly at Bravo.

"He is saying this one they look for called the Kid, is very much a man," Dominguez explained.

"Heard of him. Pretty well-known outlaw around these parts."

"A good friend of the Mexican people, I am told," Ortega said, his tone edgy. "Is such the reason why he is considered an outlaw?"

"Hardly," Starbuck replied coolly. "Happens he's killed a few men, robbed, done a lot of cattle-rustling and horse-stealing. That's what brands him an outlaw."

Ortega muttered inaudibly, turned away, and they rode on in silence. At nightfall they were deep in the towering hills, and made camp in a coulee in which there was a small spring. With daylight they were up and on the move, setting a pattern that in due time broke them out on a high ridge that had loomed before them continually for days in the distance, and started them slanting downgrade for a broad meadowland cupped in a vast mountain hollow.

Near mid-morning they intersected a well-traveled road, turned into it. Shawn pointed to a smudge of smoke hanging in the distance.

"That'll be Las Vegas. Can start thinking about that tequila you've been hankering for—along with a good restaurant meal."

"It will be a matter to celebrate!" Ortega said, evidently over his pique. He smiled, added, "The tequila, senor, not your cooking."

"Not going to hurt my feelings saying that. Fixing meals is not my long suit."

Both Mexicans looked at him, frowned, not understanding the expression. Starbuck shook his head, studied the road stretching out before them. The buildings that made up the town, booming now with the recent arrival of the railroad, were becoming visible, and the plume of smoke at that hour of the day undoubtedly was issuing from the stack of a locomotive. He hadn't been in the settlement—now divided into two sections, he'd been

120

told—for some time, guessed he'd find it much changed from the sleepy—

"Pull up!"

At the command Starbuck and the vaqueros drew to a quick halt as riders closed in on all sides of them from the brushy shoulders of the road. Surprise hit Shawn with solid force. It was Pacheco and Sandoval. With them was the Mexican soldier, and three men wearing stars.

17

"Get your hands up—fast!"

The order came from the rider in the center of the group facing them. He was a thick-shouldered, tough-looking man and wore a deputy sheriff's badge. He and the other lawmen would be from Las Vegas. Starbuck shrugged wearily, raised his arms. Sandoval and Pacheco had outguessed him again.

"These the ones?" the deputy asked impatiently, glancing at the two agents flanking him.

Pacheco nodded, a hard smile parting his lips. "Two are already dead. These three remain."

Bravo spoke sharply in Spanish. Pacheco wagged his head, replied in like tongue. The deputy shifted angrily on his saddle.

"Goddammit—talk United States so's I can savvy what you're saying!"

The Mexican nodded coldly. "Of course, Sheriff. This one complains of his innocence, that he—"

"Liar!" Dominguez broke in. "I have told him that this American is not the one who was with us in Mexico, but only a friend we have met."

The lawman scratched at his jaw in disgust. "Well, you can settle your squabbling back in town. Ain't no sense setting here in the heat arguing. . . . Take their guns, Abe, then the rest of you sort've bunch up around them, keep them in a pocket while we ride in."

An elderly man eased in beside Shawn, lifted his forty-five from its holster, moved on to perform a like chore on Ortega and Bravo. That accomplished, he pulled out of the circle and then all moved forward along the road.

The two cavalrymen were no longer members of the Mexican agent's posse, Shawn had noticed. Evidently they had been pulled off the matter, which was some degree of relief. Bucking the law was bad enough, but to go up against the army also—that was too much. How did the Mexicans know they were heading for Las Vegas? That was a puzzle and he began to mull it over thoughtfully, reviewing the hours that had passed since he had made the decision to avoid Santa Fe and cut across the mountains to the town in the meadows. There was no way, that he could see, how the information could have leaked out—but the fact remained that the two agents, with recruited reinforcements, had been waiting for them.

To assume they had acted on pure speculation

was going pretty far afield; several roads led out of the old Spanish capital—north to Taos, west to Arizona and the Utah country, northeast for the heart of the Sangre de Cristos—and of course to Las Vegas, due east. How, then, could they choose the exact one?

A low, husky mutter from Ortega drew his attention. He glanced at the vaquero to his left, frowned, then to Bravo on his right. Both were leaning forward on their saddles, with narrowed, dark eyes on the backs of the two Mexican agents riding directly in front of them.

Alarm rushed through him. The knives the vaqueros carried on their belts were missing from the scabbards. Since the man called Abe had disarmed them of only their pistols, it meant they had concealed the blades somewhere on their persons, and at the first opportunity would use them on Sandoval and Pacheco.

He leaned toward Bravo. "If you're figuring to use your knife—forget it," he whispered.

Without waiting for any response from Dominguez, Shawn turned to Ortega, repeated his warning. The big vaquero faced him sullenly.

"It is my affair, senor."

"Not quite. Means we'll all be dead if you try. Leave it up to me. Can maybe talk our way out of this."

"Talk," Ortega muttered, and spat. "Such is for nothing."

"Beats dying."

Carlos looked away, and the horses moved steadily on toward the collection of buildings that made up the town. Just how he could talk themselves out of the pocket they were in was not clear to Starbuck; in truth, he had no ideas, and little hope, but there was no chance at all if he permitted the vaqueros to go through with what they had in mind.

Best to let matters ride; something could develop, especially now that Bravo had made the statement that Shawn was not the American who had participated in the assassination of the Scorpion. That alone would have cast a shadow of doubt over the reliability of the two Mexican agents, who apparently were not too firmly established in the good graces of the Las Vegas lawman, anyway. It could make it possible for him to get a hearing for not only himself but for Bravo and Carlos as well before being surrendered to the Assassins.

They reached the end of the street—a busy, dusty thoroughfare teeming with men, women, children, and vehicles of all kinds. Somewhere up the way a locomotive hooted, sending several horses to shying nervously. Saloons were at every hand, some in tents, others in hastily erected shacks; farther on the older and more substantial area was evident through the haze.

There had been little building in the section of the flat they were moving through when he was last there, Shawn recalled; the railroad's advent, and its arbitrary bypassing of the old settlement, had given birth to a whole new town.

Bravo was talking to the Mexican soldier, a man who appeared exhausted and too far along in years to be riding in such a posse. They continued to converse while the deputy led the party through the begrudging crowds of staring people, and then Dominguez finally turned to Starbuck.

"It was of wonder to me how the *Asesinos* could be waiting in ambush for us—"

Shawn nodded. "It's a question I've been asking myself."

"There is no mystery. Zamora, the soldier, tells me that when they discovered we did not precede them on the Santa Fe road in the morning, they turn and search for us.

"They do not find us, but they encountered the lawman and those who were hunting for El Chavito—this Billy the Kid you call him. There was conversation at the water place. This you will remember."

Starbuck frowned. "Sure, but I never mentioned anything about us cutting across the mountains for Las Vegas."

"I regret to tell you, Shawn, it was Carlos. He mentioned it to one of the party, a young countryman of ours. He spoke of it later when the *Asesinos* were encountered by them and questions were asked."

Starbuck swore softly. So that was how it hap

pened. He had racked his brain for an explanation, but it had not occurred to him that it could have been one of the vaqueros who let it slip.

"Learning of this error on their part," Bravo continued, "they returned swiftly to Sante Fe, but as their horses were worn, they abandoned them and took passage on the stagecoach for Las Vegas. Thus you should not blame yourself, *compadre*, for a failure that was of our making. Had it not been Ortega's bad judgment, we now would not be in such circumstances."

Carlos, hearing his name, faced Bravo. "*Que?*"

"*Por nada*," Dominguez replied, and waved him off.

The vaquero settled back. Bravo brushed at the sweat on his dark features, gazed unseeingly out over the continually moving crowd. Both men had given up thoughts of using their knives, at least for the present, it seemed, and that relieved the worry within Shawn considerably.

What he certainly did not want was the killing of the Mexican agents, and possibly of the soldier, Zamora, hanging over the heads of the two vaqueros. He'd have no hope of pleading their case at all if such came to pass.

Questioning the authority of Pacheco and Sandoval might be the best angle. The vaqueros insisted the pair represented only a small, selfish faction of the Mexican government. Perhaps if an inquiry was placed directly to the capital in

Mexico City, one routed to a known member of the president's cabinet, a clarification of their position could be had. By making use of the army's telegraph system, it wouldn't require too much time.

If a reply indicated that the two men were not accredited representatives of the Mexican government but only of some private interest group, there would be no grounds on which the Las Vegas lawmen could hold Bravo and Ortega—and him, if they hadn't already released him on the strength of Dominguez' declaration that he was not involved.

"Head around back—"

It was the deputy's voice, giving them an order to circle the jail building.

"Pull up at the hitchrack, and set quiet till you're told to climb down."

"You want us to hang around, Jake?" one of the posse members asked as they moved into the area.

"Naw, reckon there ain't no more need. Be obliged if you'll put the horses in the barn, then you can drop your badges on my desk. I'll see you get paid."

Shawn, reining in alongside the vaqueros, waited for the word to dismount. The deputy came off first, waited while Pacheco, Sandoval, and Zamora left their saddles, and then, pistol drawn, motioned impatiently.

"All right, let's go—right through that back door there. You can cool your heels in a cell inside while I sort this thing out."

18

Their guns lay on the lawman's desk, along with the stars that had been issued men serving as deputies in the posse. Shawn, with Bravo and Carlos Ortega following, moved through the small, heat-filled room and entered the cell at its far end. There were no other prisoners.

Sandoval and Pacheco, satisfaction filling their eyes, stepped back with the clanging of the iron grill door and the snick of the lock. Zamora, rifle at his side, took up a stand at the entrance to the jail.

"It is good, Sheriff," Sandoval said.

"I ain't the sheriff, I'm the deputy," Jake replied, glancing at Zamora. "Sheriff's gone to Santa Fe. . . . Now, there ain't no need of him standing guard there," he added, jerking his head at the soldier.

"It is only a thing of habit," the agent said. "I wish to say we are grateful for your help in this matter. My government will also be grateful. We will make the arrangements to take the prisoners back at once. They will stand trial for murder."

Ortega said something sneeringly in Spanish. Jake brushed his hat to the back of his head. "Now, just hold on a minute," he drawled. "There ain't no big hurry. We'll just wait for the sheriff."

"But they are prisoners of ours. You cannot hold—"

"I sure can. This here's San Miguel County, New Mexico, and we've got the say-so far as the law's concerned."

"We have shown to you our papers—"

"Ain't denying that, but the sheriff'll have to see them, too. Pretty sure he'll turn the prisoners over to you, all right, but I still got to go through the motions of letting him do the deciding."

Pacheco, face glistening with sweat, stared sullenly at the vaqueros through the bars. Sandoval raised his hands, let them fall helplessly to his sides.

"There is no need for such, senor! And we wish to begin the return journey to Mexico this day. To wait will be a great inconvenience, as we must travel by stagecoach."

The deputy wagged his head. "Well, I'm mighty sorry about it, *amigo,* but that's how it's going to be. Can't see why one more day'll make such a powerful difference."

"Perhaps there is fear that inquiry concerning them will be made by your sheriff," Bravo suggested. "Such could be the reason for haste."

Sandoval spat out an answer to Dominguez in Spanish. Bravo only smiled, his eyes on the lawman.

"You claiming they ain't real agents of the Mex government?" he asked.

"They are *Asesinos*—assassins," Ortega snapped. "As such they are known throughout Mexico."

"Yeah, but are they working for your government?"

"That is something you should learn for yourself."

"Goddammit!" the deputy exploded. "Cut out all this hemming and hawing and beating about the bush and say what you mean!" Shifting his attention to Shawn, leaning against the back wall of the cell, he added, "Any chance of getting a straight answer from you?"

"He knows nothing of the affair of which we are accused," Bravo said. "We have an acquaintance of only a few days—since El Paso."

"A lie!" Pacheco shouted angrily. "He is the American who was the leader of the men who murdered General Jaramillo!"

"It is you who lies," Dominguez replied quietly. "He is aiding us in the search for that American. We believe him to be in Dodge City. We engaged the senor to take us there."

"That right?" Jake demanded. He was well over his depth in a complicated situation and it turned him angry.

"That's the way it is."

"That also is a lie!" Sandoval protested. "We found this man with the murderers, in El Paso where they had all fled. When we attempted to arrest Dominguez, they together escaped. Later there was another attempt to arrest them at the place of an Indian village ruin. He fought by their side. One of my men was killed and a soldier of yours assigned to us for our use in El Paso was wounded."

The lawman was studying Starbuck narrowly. "What've you got to say to that?"

"Pretty much the way it was, only—"

"You admitting you sided them two vaqueros they're claiming murdered that general?"

"Way I see it, they aren't murderers in the real sense of the word. Hard to make you understand what I mean, I know, but if you heard the whole story I expect you'd look at it the same way I do."

Jake sat down on the edge of his desk. Outside in the street the rumble and rattle of traffic continued without letup. The man who had taken charge of the horses entered, sank onto one of the benches placed along the wall. Mopping at the sweat on his forehead, he said, "God, it sure is a hot one, ain't it?"

Starbuck smiled at the deputy. "If you don't mind taking a suggestion," he said gently, "it'd be smart check with the Mexican authorities. I've got my doubts these two men work for the government in Mexico City."

"Ain't got the authority to do that," the deputy said at once. "Have to leave it up to the sheriff."

Shawn stirred indifferently. "Just so somebody does. You going to keep me locked up? Can prove I wasn't in Mexico at the time that general was killed, if you'll give me the chance."

Confined to a cell there was nothing at all he

could do for Bravo and Carlos Ortega; free to move about, there was the possibility that he could enlist aid for their cause.

"You will not free him!" Sandoval cried, surging toward the deputy.

Jake waved the man back. "Hell, no, I ain't turning him loose," he said, and nodded to Starbuck. "Like as not you ain't no more mixed up in this mess than you claim, but it'll still be up to the sheriff to say what'll be done."

Pacheco had stepped up to Sandoval's side, spoken quietly to him. The agent nodded, faced the deputy.

"Is there not a *magistrado*—what you would call a judge—that we may talk to and who can issue the proper paper to release these prisoners to us?"

Jake gave that consideration. "Well, yeah, reckon you could go see Judge Romero."

The face of the agent brightened. "Romero? He is a Mexican?"

"Mexican or Spanish, I wouldn't be knowing."

"Where is he to be found?"

"Across the bridge in old town. Have to ask somebody on the street when you get there. Office is sort of hard to find."

"*Gracias.* We will locate him, and bring back to you the authority for releasing these men to us. *Adios.*"

Such was entirely possible, Shawn thought. Both Ortega and Bravo Dominguez were Mexican nationals, and the Assassins had warrants authorizing them to arrest and return them to Mexico. Romero would probably accept their credentials without question and issue a release instructing the deputy to turn them over for transference to their native land—along with him as an accessory to the murder. If there was only a way to get word to Romero, insist that he investigate first—but how?

"I'll be waiting right here," Jake said.

The agents moved to the doorway, stepped out into the driving sunlight. Pacheco paused, said something in a low voice to Zamora. The soldier bobbed, continued to stand at attention.

Jake grinned. "Told you to stay put, keep an eye on them, that it?"

Zamora frowned, not understanding.

"Well, you don't need to be worrying none. They ain't going nowheres," the deputy said, rising and hanging a ring of keys on a wall peg. "Leastwise they ain't until the sheriff gets here or Judge Romero tells me to hand them over to your friends."

The soldier bobbed again, agreeing to what he assumed were approving words. The second deputy rose, walked to the doorway, halted as Jake settled himself into the swivel chair behind the desk. Somewhere in the settlement two gunshots sounded in quick succession above the ordinary din, but the lawmen did not seem to notice.

Starbuck glanced at Ortega and Bravo. They were slumped on the hard, wooden cot, backs

133

against the wall. Their faces were expressionless, and it would seem they had resigned themselves to the prospect of being escorted back to Mexico, while in their minds they would be making plans to escape at the first opportunity.

But for himself—and for them—he was not giving up. Regardless of an order from a judge giving custody of them to Sandoval and Pacheco, he intended to—

"Sheriff!"

The summons came from the street, accompanied by pounding footsteps. Jake rose hastily, crossed to the doorway, and halted beside the other deputy, who had turned about and was looking off into the distance.

"Sheriff ain't here," he said. "Only Pete and me. What's the trouble?"

"Doc Holliday just shot and killed Mike Gordon," the man replied between gasps for breath. "You sure better come quick!"

Jake wheeled, snatched up a shotgun, and hurried into the open. "C'mon, Pete!" he shouted.

19

"Escape—it must come now!"

Carlos Ortega's words were low, insistent. Outside in the street people were hurrying by, anxious to reach the scene of the excitement. Zamora, curiosity aroused, had stepped into the open.

"It is so," Bravo agreed. "This *magistrado*, Romero, I have the feeling he will not be a friend. What are your thoughts, Shawn?"

Starbuck nodded. Their best chances for being cleared lay in Dodge City where he could outline their predicament to a lawman with whom he was acquainted—Wyatt Earp. Here in Las Vegas, among strangers, it was likely they would be accorded short shrift.

"I'm all for it," he said, glancing toward the door, "but we're going to have to move fast—and the only way out of this cell is by a key."

He glanced at the ring hanging from its wall peg, frowned, pivoted to the vaqueros. "That soldier—Zamora—can you get him in here?" he asked in an urgent voice.

"I can do so," Ortega replied at once. "You have a plan?"

Starbuck pointed to the keys. "Call him in close, then put your knife to his throat. Tell him he's dead unless he does what we tell him."

Ortega stepped to the front of the cell. "Zamora, *por favor!*"

The soldier turned, looked back into the room. Carlos brushed feebly at his eyes, beckoned.

"Es importante—"

Zamora shifted his rifle to his left hand, walked back into the room. People were no longer hurrying past in the direction of the shooting, and Shawn knew that now, with each fading moment,

135

their opportunity for escape was diminishing. Tense, he watched the soldier move up to the bars, question in his dark eyes.

"*Que quieres?*"

"*Esta,*" Ortega answered, and pulling his knife from inside his shirt, pressed the sharp point against the man's throat, while with his free hand he held him tight against the bars. A half smile on his lips, he turned to Starbuck.

"The pigeon is yours, senor."

Shawn was already beside him. "Tell him to take his rifle, reach out with it and hook that ring of keys on the end of the barrel—"

Bravo, drawing his blade as further persuasion, pushed its point into the back of the soldier's neck and waited while Carlos relayed the command. Then he added words of his own.

Zamora did not hesitate. Holding his head rigid to relieve the prick of the knives, he extended the rifle, dislodged the ring with the sight at the end of the barrel, and let it slide down to his hand.

Instantly Starbuck reached through the bars, pulled the circle of thick wire from the weapon, and crossed to the cell door. Inserting the correct key in the lock, he released it. The grillwork swung open and he hurriedly stepped through, followed quickly by Bravo.

Ortega, blade still held to the throat of the frightened Zamora, did not move. Moving fast, Shawn disarmed the man, shoved him into the cell.

Zamora fell onto the cot, faced Ortega, and said something in an earnest tone to the vaquero.

"He begs us not to kill him," Bravo explained as Starbuck, retrieving their pistols from the top of the desk, handed him his weapon.

"Don't," Shawn said. "He was only following orders. Just lock him in."

"But will he not make an outcry?"

"He will not," Ortega said calmly, and taking his pistol from Starbuck, swung it at the soldier's head. Zamora slumped back onto the cot. Holstering the gun, the vaquero nodded to Starbuck.

"He will be silent for a time. What is next?"

"The horses," Shawn answered, hurrying toward the rear exit of the jail. "We'll find them in that barn out back."

Opening the door cautiously, he glanced about. The weathered structure where their mounts had been taken was a dozen yards or more farther on. Two men were standing at the corner of the building, their attention on something down the street—the shooting, most likely.

"Let's go," Starbuck murmured, and stepping into the open, quickly crossed the yard.

He reached the wide entrance to the stable, with Bravo and Ortega close behind. Entering the shadow-filled structure, he paused. The hostler was probably among the crowd gathered in the street—but there was the possibility that he had returned, and it was only smart to be sure.

"Find the horses," he said quietly to the vaqueros, and as they moved past him, he stepped over to a room on his left that evidently served as an office. He peered carefully into it, sighed. It was the hostler's combination quarters and office, and it was empty. The stableman was still out in the street.

Wheeling, Starbuck hurried along the runway, his glance probing the dark areas as he searched for the sorrel. The two men lounging at the corner of the barn worried him—they could have some connection with the stable, the owners, perhaps, or possibly customers, and could put in an appearance at any moment. The same applied to Jake and the other deputy—

"Here, senor, your horse."

At Bravo's whispered summons, Shawn walked quickly to the stall where the gelding was contentedly munching hay. As he began to throw his gear into place, he saw Ortega in the adjoining compartment getting his mount saddled. Evidently Bravo's black was in the space beyond him.

Finished, Shawn backed the gelding into the runway, looking first to the wide door through which they had entered, and then to the rear of the building. Through that opening he could see nearby buildings, making it of little consequence which route they chose for departure.

Bravo and Carlos, holding the reins of their mounts, moved up beside him.

"Out the back," he said, swinging onto the saddle. "If luck's with us nobody'll notice."

"The luck will be theirs—and not good," Ortega said grimly. "I will not again be put in a jail."

Starbuck urged the sorrel toward the doorway. He wanted to tell Carlos that killing someone at that time was the worst possible thing he could do, but it seemed pointless. The vaquero was determined not to be taken back to Mexico, where certain death awaited him, and thus a caution of such nature would mean nothing to him.

Reaching the doorway, he halted. From his height on the saddle he could look over the corrals and fences, see the crowd assembled several hundred yards down the street. The excitement was over, and bystanders were already turning away, resuming whatever they had been doing when it all began.

The stable's rear exit let out into an alleyway that led directly to the street. He was reluctant to chance such a course since it would take them straight into people returning to the center of town, but there was no alternative; it would be no different now in the front of the jail.

"We must hurry, senor—"

At Bravo's anxious words, Shawn nodded. "When we come to those buildings at the end of the alley," he said, pointing, "turn right. Take it slow and easy. Want to make it look like we're just riding through."

Roweling the sorrel lightly, he moved out, Ortega to his left, Bravo Dominguez on the right. They walked their horses slowly, making little sound and drawing no attention. Once they were out of the narrow lane and in the street, their passage should be less marked since they would be mingling with others, both on foot and mounted. In the deserted alley they stood out prominently.

The entrance into the street, a gateway formed by structures on either side, was immediately ahead. Starbuck felt his muscles tighten. This would be the moment of danger, the time when they rode into view of any and all who were nearby; he could only hope that among those who noticed would not be Jake or Pete, or any of the other deputies who were in the posse.

Shawn, suddenly tense, slowed the sorrel's pace even more and swung farther to the right side of the alley in order to make a close turn. Bravo eased in behind him, and Ortega, near the center of the lane, began to follow.

Abruptly the vaquero halted. In that same fragment of time Starbuck caught motion at the corner of the building to his left, paused.

"It is them!"

Alarm shot through Starbuck. The voice was that of Pacheco. The Mexican agent was standing at the end of the alley. Beside him was Sandoval. Evidently they had met with the judge, were hurrying back to the jail.

Shawn saw Pacheco reach for the pistol on his hip. Sandoval dropped to one knee, clawed for his weapon also. Jamming spurs savagely into the sorrel's flanks, he sent the big gelding plunging straight for the older man. From the corner of an eye he saw Ortega launch himself from the saddle at Pacheco. Mindful of the need to attract as little attention as possible, the vaquero was avoiding the use of his gun and had his knife in hand instead.

There was a muffled report as Pacheco's pistol fired. The sorrel, refusing to run down Sandoval, veered sharply. Starbuck lashed out with a booted foot, caught the Mexican on the side of the head, bowling him over.

Shouts were rising in the street, and he could hear the pound of boot heels as he wheeled to aid Ortega. The vaquero lay face up, sightless eyes staring into the sky. Blood covered his shirt front, bubbled from a wound Pacheco's bullet had inflicted in his chest. Nearby Pacheco lay dead also, Ortega's knife driven to the hilt in his throat.

"Shawn—"

Bravo's urgent call brought Starbuck around. The crowd was closing in, shouting, pointing. Someone was calling for the deputy. Casting a quick look at Sandoval, stirring groggily, Shawn again roweled the sorrel, and with Bravo Dominguez a length ahead, raced for the end of the alley, and the street.

20

Gunshots racketed through the hot, dust-filled air as they rounded the building standing to their right and entered the street. Jake and Pete—and possibly some of the other special deputies—had answered the crowd's summons and had recognized them. Bent low, he glanced at Bravo. The vaquero had turned, was looking back toward the alley where Carlos Ortega lay dead.

"*Vaya a Dios, companero,*" Shawn heard him say.

A dog, attracted by the pounding hooves of the horses, rushed out from a yard, barking furiously. Ignoring the animal, Starbuck raised himself slightly, looked ahead. They had left the buildings of the settlement behind, were now on the road that led eventually to Fort Union. Such was only a matter of necessity, a fact that would be altered as soon as they reached the trees a short distance farther on and were no longer visible to anyone in pursuit. The last thing they wanted was to ride into an army post with a posse at their heels.

The pursuit was already under way. Glancing back as he and the deeply silent Dominguez reached the first of the cottonwoods and other trees, he saw a dozen or so riders strung out in their wake. Leading the party was the deputy, Jake, and the man nearby, he thought, was Sandoval. He and

Dominguez were beyond range of any weapon, pistol or rifle, so there was no cause for alarm on that point. Their immediate concern was maintaining the lead they had seized until they could shake the posse entirely.

Well into the grove, Starbuck began to veer the sorrel to the right. The Canadian River was somewhere east of them, and once there he could get his bearings and make definite plans. It was a fair distance to the stream, however, he recalled.

"Keep in the trees!" he shouted to Bravo as the sunlit area of a clearing began to show through the growth ahead of them.

Dominguez, features stilled, nodded slightly, guided his black away from the meadowlike area. They circled it at a fast run. Beyond it, Shawn threw a glance over his shoulder once more. The horses were beginning to tire and soon the pace would have to be slowed. There was no sign of the lawman and his posse. It was just possible they had continued on northeast through the grove toward Fort Union, had missed where he and Bravo had turned off.

He began to draw in the gelding, slow his stride. Foam flecked the coats of both mounts, and Bravo's black was trembling from exertion. Shawn pointed to a low hill covered with cedars.

"Can stop there, breathe the horses," he called above the thud of hooves. "Like to see if we've lost Jake and his friends, too."

Bravo's reply was only a nod. A man undeniably accustomed to death, that of Carlos Ortega was hitting him hard, considerably more so than had that of Gomez, and Starbuck was finding it difficult to understand. He had thought Francisco and Bravo much closer than either of them was to Ortega.

It was possible that Francisco, being a wholly self-sufficient man, caused no worries, while Carlos, impetuous and entirely unpredictable, was one the others felt a need to look out for—just as the wayward sheep straying from the fold receives the most attention.

They reached the hill, swung into the squat cedars, dismounted. Shawn, wheeling to climb to the crest, paused, faced Bravo.

"Like to say I'm sorry about Carlos—"

Dominguez was staring off into the distance. "It was as he would wish," he murmured.

Starbuck continued on to the top of the hill, and taking care to remain concealed, turned his attention to the west. He swore softly. The posse had not been sidetracked; they were at that very moment skirting the clearing and advancing toward them.

Pulling back, he returned to where Bravo waited with the horses. "We didn't lose them—they're headed this way right now. Coming slow, but coming just the same."

Dominguez made no comment, wheeled to his

horse, and went to the saddle. Shawn crossed to the sorrel, also mounted, and pulled about. Both horses were still sucking for wind but it would be risky to delay any further. Jake and his party were too close; best they move on, even if at a more deliberate pace, and keep ahead of the riders. Apparently the deputy was depending entirely upon tracking the two horses for guidance.

That conclusion brought an idea to Starbuck. Saying nothing to Dominguez in the way of explanation, he cut back due south through the trees and brush, taking the usual care to not become exposed, and made a wide circle that returned them to the clearing. At that point, Bravo, recognizing ground over which they had previously passed, called softly to him.

"Senor, have we become lost?"

Shawn grinned. "Just giving that posse a little extra tracking to do," he replied, and continued on, riding over the same hoof prints their horses had left in the soil a short time earlier, and that Jake and his men were at that moment engaged in following.

Thus it became a matter of the pursuers being pursued, and for the length of a wide circle, while their horses gradually recovered their strength at the slow pace, Shawn and the vaquero played a tense game. Reaching the hill for a second time, Starbuck lifted his hand in a signal to halt. Without dismounting, he rode to the top of the mound to a point where he could look out over the land to the south and west.

Satisfaction stirred him. The posse, members of which were near enough to be easily identifiable, had taken the bait, were circling back toward the clearing. At once he returned to Bravo.

"They fell for it," he said as they moved out. "Right now they're doubling back to the clearing—probably figure we're heading for town. By the time they get it all ironed out we ought to have a long lead on them. . . . Sandoval was there. Guess he wasn't bad hurt."

"He has such good fortune," Dominguez murmured.

They rode on steadily, now taking a true northeast course for the Cimarron Cutoff which would lead them eventually into Kansas and Dodge City.

A time later they reached a fair-sized stream and halted. It was not the Canadian, Starbuck was certain; they had not traveled far enough yet to reach it, according to his calculations. Too, this was a much smaller river.

Leaving Bravo with the horses in the cool shade, Shawn backtracked a short distance to a lightning-struck pine he'd noted in passing. He climbed up its scorched trunk to where he had a good view of the surrounding country. Ahead the trail looked much the same—and to the rear there were no riders in sight for as far as he could see. They had finally rid themselves of the posse. Pleased, he descended to the ground and retraced his steps to the vaquero.

"Looks like we've lost them," he said.

Bravo smiled wearily. "I have thought it no longer matters greatly."

Starbuck settled on a grassy hummock in the shadow of an oak, and mopping the sweat from his face, studied Dominguez narrowly.

"That another way of saying you're giving it up?"

The vaquero shrugged in the customary fashion of his people when no reply was necessary.

"Ortega getting killed—that what's causing you to change your mind?"

Bravo picked up a handful of loose dirt, allowed it to trickle through his fingers. From the top of a nearby rock a striped ground squirrel eyed them with hard, bright interest.

"First Felipe, and then Francisco. Now it is Carlos. I am thinking this was not to be."

"Not that at all. Just the price you're having to pay."

"But three of four of us are dead. That is a very high price."

"Got to admit it is, but on the other hand, what you're paying it for is worth plenty—a whole village, families, their homes, those haciendas in the Joaquin Valley you told me about. You losing sight of what it will mean if we can find Amigo and collect your money's so that you can return and put things right?"

Dominguez, features expressionless, watched the last of the sandy soil spill from his hand.

"Without doubt it would be what you call in your language a salvation for many," he agreed quietly, "but I fear it will never come to pass. There is too much misfortune, and good is always overcome by evil, it appears."

"Hard to figure out why that sometimes happens," Starbuck said, scrubbing at the whiskers thickening on his jaw. "Wondered about it myself plenty and never could find a good answer. All I ever decided was that no matter how bad things got, a man has to keep on doing what he knows is right."

Bravo gave that considerable thought, finally stirred and drew himself upright. Turning to Shawn, he smiled.

"Forgive my moment of weakness, good friend. It was only that Carlos and I were as brothers— from the day of birth, almost. Such applies also with Francisco and Felipe, and I know that what we began I must finish."

"Didn't figure you'd back off once you thought it over. . . . Losing a good friend can set you to wondering, though."

"Of a certainty. Will we camp here?"

Shawn rose, moved to the sorrel. "No, we keep riding," he answered, mounting. "Had hoped we could make it to the Canadian by dark."

"It is too far for such?"

148

"Not sure. Times before when I rode through here I was farther north. About all we can do is keep riding until we come to it."

Bravo agreed to that bit of practical wisdom, and swinging onto his black, moved up beside Shawn. They forded the stream together, gained the solid ground beyond, and continued on their way. Instead of halting for a noon meal, they snacked on dried meat and hard biscuits from their dwindling supply of food, stopping only to rest the horses.

They saw no more of the posse and it did seem they had shaken it, but it was not in Starbuck to lower his guard entirely. Several times, as the day wore on, he raised himself in the stirrups, twisted about, and searched the trail behind them for indications of riders, always finding none.

The country was changing gradually. They were pulling away from the high mountains, were entering a land of rolling, grass-covered hills dotted here and there with scrub cedars. The black scar of lava beds etched the surface in places, and the deep arroyos were rocky, had more the look of a permanent stream bed except that there was no water. It was good cattle country but no stock was in evidence and Shawn pondered the lack.

It could be an Indian problem—and of course No Man's Land, that outlaw haven lying between Kansas and the Indian Territory, was not too distant. Raising beef in the area could be a profitless venture.

"There is a river," Bravo called, pointing. "Can it be this Canadian of which you speak?"

Starbuck glanced to the west. The sun was down and only its fading amber glow filled the sky. He hadn't realized it was so late.

"Have to be," he replied. "No other river around here."

"It is here you wish to camp—"

"Yeah, on the other side in the trees. Come morning we'll head straight north. Can't be more than twenty-five miles now to where we'll hit the Cutoff."

21

Voices, loud and argumentative, awoke Starbuck the next morning. He lay quiet for a time as he sought to determine their source, concluded that they came from across the river, and sat up.

Bravo had roused also. "It is the posse—"

"Could be," Starbuck said, and got to his feet.

Moving to the edge of the trees, he peered through the screening brush. There were five men—and it was the posse. He recognized the deputy, Jake, immediately. The lawman was slumped forward on his saddle, speaking angrily to a man squatting at the edge of the water. Apparently he was the one doing the tracking for the party, had lost the trail and was now taking a tongue lashing from Jake for his inability. Shawn stirred impatiently. He'd thought they were finally rid of the lawman, but it seemed he had been wrong. He was glad now that he'd taken the trouble to double back on foot after they'd crossed the river and wipe out the tracks of the horses.

"The Assassin—I do not see him."

Bravo had approached so quietly that Shawn had not become aware of the vaquero's presence until he moved in beside him. Frowning, he looked more closely at the riders. It was true; Sandoval was not in the party.

"Bunch must've split up and he's with the others, or else he's quit and gone back to town. Jake had more men with him yesterday."

"Sandoval will not quit. That you should know by now."

"No, guess he won't. Can't see why Jake would divide his posse, however. Knew we were ahead of him and all he had to do was try to catch up."

The vaquero shrugged. "There is little reason, but where is Sandoval—and the others?"

"Might've been hurt worse than we figured, and had to go back. My sorrel was moving pretty fast when I hit him. Would've been a mighty hard wallop. Far as the others are concerned, they probably got tired and headed for home. Volunteers in a posse are that way. Pull out whenever they take the notion."

Dominguez considered that in his quiet way, eyes on the men across the stream. They had dismounted, were now stalking about, stretching, relieving their muscles. The tracker, sucking indifferently on a pipe, seemed oblivious to them or the words of the deputy.

"Such would seem to be the facts," Bravo agreed, finally. "He is hurt, cannot ride."

"Which is one thing we'd better do," Starbuck said hurriedly. "That tracker will get his thinking done in a few more minutes, ford the stream, and start working this side. By the time he runs into something that'll tip him off we want to be plenty far from here."

Wheeling, with Bravo at his side, he dropped back to where their horses were picketed. Together, quietly, they collected their gear and saddled their mounts. Then, leading the horses, they moved off into the trees. Deep in the grove and away from the river where there would be no danger of being seen, they swung aboard and struck a course due north.

Riding fast, they quickly left the area of the Canadian behind and soon were in a country broken by buttes and deep arroyos, and studded with bayonet yucca, rabbitbush, sage, patches of purple thistle, and cactus. An occasional cottonwood broke the low profile of the prairie growth.

Starbuck pulled up near mid-morning in a small sink where a lone tree, fed by an underground stream, spread a canopy of shade. Although there had been no sign of pursuit, they had not taken time to eat since leaving the Canadian, and both were feeling the need for food. Staking out the horses on the good grass, they prepared a meal as best they could from their limited larder.

When they were finishing the last of their coffee, Bravo rolled himself a cigarette and said, "The posse—will it not halt? It was my understanding that the authority of such a party did not go beyond the border of its own territory."

"Still in New Mexico," Starbuck explained. "Once we cross over into No Man's Land, Jake'll likely pull off. He will for sure when we get to Kansas. His New Mexico badge is no good there."

"This No Man's Land—why is it so called?"

"It's a strip of country nobody claims—or seems to want. Outlaw hangout, mostly, and a lawman's pushing his luck when he goes there."

"Can he not arrest an outlaw there?"

"Sure, if he's got the guts. It's been done—but usually by somebody with a big posse, well-armed, backing him."

"What of the deputy? He will try, you think, if we are found there?"

Starbuck's shoulders stirred. "Don't know him well enough to say. My guess is he'll turn back when he comes to the border."

"If this does not prove to be so, how far will we be from Kansas?"

"Day's ride, more or less."

Bravo sighed, flipped his cigarette into the ashes

of the fire. "This country—it is much like my Mexico. Always it is a very long way to anywhere."

Starbuck grinned, got to his feet, and began preparations to ride on.

"Can we not mount and ride fast and get to Dodge City soon?"

Shawn paused at the vaquero's question. "Like you said, it's a far piece to anywhere—and a mile's a mile no matter how you figure it. But we can push hard."

"Such would please me greatly, *compadre*. I am anxious to get this journey completed and be on the way back to my country. Each day the difficulties in the Joaquin Valley grow worse; of that I am sure."

Shawn nodded. "I understand. Starting now it'll be up to the horses. We'll go as fast and as far every day as they can stand."

Shortly they were again in the saddle and resuming the trail, now bearing northeast. They caught a glimpse of the posse—small, dark marks in the far distance—and not long after they reached the Santa Fe Trail Cutoff and were following its deeply rutted trace.

Jake and his men were well behind and it was doubtful they could have seen the two fugitives they had set out to overtake. Too, lacking the presence of Cruz Sandoval, the determination to pursue them undoubtedly wavered, and not too

154

much more effort was likely to be expended. But, cautious as always, Starbuck elected to run no risks.

"Don't see how they can possibly get even close to us," he said to Bravo when they paused to rest the horses, "but we won't give them a chance. Aim to keep on going long as we can."

"The border—will we come to there by sundown?"

"No, still going to have a half a day's ride in front of us."

They camped that night on the crest of a high bluff, a position that enabled them to look out over the land across which they had ridden and to locate eventually the campfire of the posse. Jake had also continued for a time after darkness fell, but he too had been forced to halt finally.

"Guess you can say we've got him licked now," Starbuck said as they rolled up in their blankets. For the first time he had no doubts as to their being able to escape the posse. "By noon tomorrow we'll be in No Man's Land—and the next day it'll be Kansas. . . . Too much ground between us now for him to ever catch up."

Dominguez sighed. "It has been a long ride, one of many happenings—and death. I am now the last of those who killed El Escorpion, except for Amigo, and I pray to the Virgin that I may live to undo some of the wrongs he and his soldiers have committed."

"You will," Shawn assured him. "We'll make it to Dodge and track down this Amigo and collect the money he owes you—along with what's due your partners—then head back for Mexico. With ten thousand dollars you can do a lot of good."

"True, but there is nothing I can do for those who are dead."

"Can't look at it that way, Bravo. Sure, a man doesn't ever want to forget them, but he's got to bear in mind that there's no way he can bring them back. Only answer is to go ahead and do what he can for the living, and do it in their memory. . . . Get some sleep, my friend. Tomorrow'll be a tough day."

It was one of many hours, and while they now had no fear of the posse, they pushed the horses to their limits, nevertheless.

In the succeeding two days, ignoring personal weariness, they crossed the panhandle of unwanted territory and rode into Kansas. Pausing only briefly, they pressed on across the gently rolling country until a settlement was encountered. There they replenished food stock, tarried a short time in the interests of their fagged mounts, and again rode on.

On the evening of the fourth day as they made camp Starbuck nodded to Dominguez and said, "Be the last time we'll do this for a spell. By noon tomorrow we'll be in Dodge City."

22

"*Manana*," Bravo murmured distantly as they sat by the fire a time later. "This tomorrow has been long in coming."

"Has at that," Starbuck agreed, "and there's been something I've wanted to tell you before we got there. Intended to do it sooner but things kept pushing us and a good chance never did turn up."

"It is of importance?"

"Expect you'll think so. There's a possibility this Amigo is my brother."

The vaquero drew himself up slowly. "Your brother? This is something you have believed from the beginning?"

"Got to be honest with you—I've had the feeling they could be the same man ever since you told me about him. My brother now calls himself Friend, and your man's name is Amigo. Could be a connection."

"There are other reasons also?"

"Can think of a few."

"Then it is likely so," Bravo said thoughtfully. "Was this in your mind when you volunteered to conduct us to Dodge City?"

"It was—leastwise it was part of it. Aimed to pull out anyway, however, and throwing in with you and Carlos and Francisco just sort of fell into line."

"This brother—"

"His real name's Ben."

"This Ben, it was your plan to protect him from us should it become necessary for us to kill him?"

Shawn's shoulders moved slightly. "Hoped to avoid anything like that. If it came to a showdown, I'd have no choice."

"Then we are to be enemies—"

Starbuck reached for the tin of coffee, refilled his cup. "Don't have to be," he said, "and I sure don't want it to be that way. I figure if Amigo is Ben, and he has your gold, I can make him turn it over to you without any gunplay."

Bravo shook his head. "I am doubtful of that. He is not one who will part with gold so easily. . . . That he can be your brother I find difficult to believe. There is much difference between you in heart."

"Can't say about that, or anything else where he's concerned. Haven't seen him in over a dozen years."

"And you were but a small one then—thus you are not acquainted at all."

"Right. I've been trying to find him ever since Pa died. Trailed him all over the country, never been lucky enough to catch up."

"There is trouble between you?"

"No. . . . Need him so's I can settle Pa's estate. There's money involved, not a big lot of it—and it's taking me so long to straighten it all out that I'm getting to where the cash doesn't really count for much anymore. I just want to get things cleared up so's I can start living like other folks, have a life of my own."

Dominguez was silent for a time. Then, "It is to be regretted that any man can come between us. I have felt honored to call you my friend and—"

"Could be we're moving a little fast. Not sure Amigo is Ben, only think it's possible."

"It is most likely since the names are of the same nature. I must tell you this, Shawn. I have my duty to perform, my obligation to my companions and to myself—"

"Know that, but you've got to understand that I can't stand by and let my own brother get killed, either. No need for it, anyway. All that I'm asking is that you let me talk to him first."

Again the Mexican was silent. After a time he rose, walked to the edge of the camp, and beyond the reach of the fire's glare, looked out over the broad prairie to the west, rippling silver now as a breeze stirred the moonlight-flooded short grass. Finally he wheeled, returned, and still standing, faced Starbuck.

"It is agreed. As a friend closer than any brother, I can do no less than permit you to have your wish. We shall seek out Amigo, and if he is your Ben, you will have the opportunity to persuade him to right the wrong he has committed. If he does not agree, then it is entirely my affair. Are we thus in accord?"

"We are," Starbuck answered slowly, "but there's one thing. If Amigo's not Ben, you'd better go a bit slow. You can't just up and kill a man without a good reason."

"Is not the fact that he has taken gold that belonged to others, and is therefore a thief, reason enough?"

"It's a good one, all right, only you'll have to let the law handle it."

The vaquero sighed heavily, sat down. "Again we must consider your law. You have a strange justice which does not permit a man to right a wrong done him or protect himself and his property! I have heard of killings—"

"It's a little hard to explain. Man can protect himself with a gun—we call it self-defense, but—"

"But he is not allowed to punish one who has wronged him in a serious way! It is beyond me. Do you have acquaintance with a lawman in Dodge to whom you can explain my need?"

"Happens I do know one. Name's Wyatt Earp. He's straight and I think he'll listen, do all he can to help you. He'd want you to swear out a warrant so's he could arrest Amigo, then the matter would go to court—"

"Court! There is no time for courts—and I, a Mexican in a country of Americans, what justice could I expect? It is said—"

"Forget what's said! No matter who or what you

are, every man gets a fair hearing in our courts. Country was built on that kind of a promise."

Dominguez said nothing, merely shook his head. A coyote yapped into the night, and from the darkness beyond the fire's glare, the eyes of some small, curious creature glowed like two small rubies.

"This Wyatt Earp, would it not then be wise to meet first with him?" Bravo asked after a time.

"That's what I figure we ought to do," Starbuck said, relieved. The vaquero had apparently decided to heed his warning, be reasonable. "Thought we could ride in, look up Earp, and ask him about Amigo. He'll know if somebody's moved in recently, loaded with gold, and opened up a new saloon, or bought out an old one. Can save a lot of chasing around."

"It is a good plan."

Shawn frowned. "One thing's just occurred to me. There's a chance that Las Vegas deputy, Jake, has sent a telegram to the marshal in Dodge about us. Nobody back there knew me by name, so if I ride in to see Earp alone nobody'll suspect anything—"

"I understand. If we are together, and being that I am Mexican, they will know instantly that we are those who were engaged in breaking out of jail and the killing that happened in Las Vegas."

"Exactly. Means I best go see Earp alone. You can wait for me at the edge of town."

"A wise plan. . . . If Amigo is your brother and is agreeable to giving back the gold that is ours, what then will you do? You have said that there is this important business of your father's that must be taken care of."

Shawn gave that a moment's thought, decided they were looking a bit far ahead, naming a colt before it was even foaled; such could wait until they knew for certain if Ben and Amigo were one and the same, but he realized what it was that disturbed Bravo.

"I made a deal with you," he said, "and I'll keep it. However it works out, I'll see you back to Mexico."

Dominguez relaxed visibly. The thought of transporting ten thousand dollars in gold back across a country with which he was unfamiliar, alone, was troubling him deeply.

"You are a man of honor, senor."

Starbuck shrugged. "Gave you my word. Was taught to live up to it."

"Such is why I cannot believe Amigo is this brother for whom you search. He would possess no such feeling of obligation."

"Can't see Ben as a man who'd double-cross you and the others, myself, but then I keep remembering that I don't really know him anymore. Things happen to people, cause them to change."

"Truly so. I think back to the Joaquin Valley—to my family, my good friends, and to what has overtaken us. No longer is life pleasant, a joy. Now it is grim and we have become bitter and mistrustful, and no one cares to look to the future."

"If you get that gold back you can go a long way toward changing that. I know you can't make it like it was—a man never can, no matter how hard he tries—but just putting forth the effort will give folks the heart to start over."

"Such is my hope. Shawn, if I die as have the others, will you take the gold back to Mexico for me? There is a girl there in our village—the name of Celestina. Explain all to her. She will know what is to be done."

Starbuck said, "You've got my promise," and rising, crossed to where his canteen hung from a tree limb. Pulling the cork, he helped himself to a drink. Nearby the horses stirred wearily.

Could Amigo and Ben be the same person? He'd know before too long, now, and if it proved to be the fact, the long quest would be ended. . . .

23

The day broke warm and cloudy, with the smell of rain riding the light wind. Breakfast was a quiet affair, only a few words passing between the two men, and shortly after sunrise they were in the saddle and moving up the well-worn road to Dodge City.

There were other travelers, all westbound, some in

canvas-topped Conestogas bearing entire families and their possessions, heavily loaded farm wagons, buggies, men on horseback, even a few undertaking the journey to whatever destination they had in mind on foot. The exodus seemed continual.

"These people, where do they go?" Bravo wondered. "Have they been driven from their homes—as have many in my country?"

"Not so much that—war we went through ended about fifteen years ago. It's just that there's a lot of unsettled land in the West. They're looking for a better life and figure they'll find it there."

"A better life is what my people hope for also," the vaquero said. "Once it was to be easily found and enjoyed, and there was no thought of it ending. But change came and we lost all. Others, such as El Escorpion, gained much."

"Can't see that he's much ahead—"

"Because he no longer lives? True, he personally, but Jaramillo is only the symbol of many. Where he paid for his greed with his life, there are thousands who have not and who have stolen our heritage and our way of life—that of the *patron*, the *hacendado*.

"I do not resent those who were poor and who now have full bellies, a roof to protect them from the sun, walls to turn away the cold winds. I resent the Jaramillos who have deceived and betrayed the peons in the name of freedom and have taken all for themselves.

"Men such as they care nothing for the poor peon. To them he is only something by which to gain power and wealth, a nothing who will die of his own incompetence in a land where nature gives but grudgingly. It is only pity for those that is in my heart. It is for those who have brought such about that I find hate. . . . Do you understand?"

Starbuck nodded, shrugged. "Change is hard on everybody—the people that caused it and the ones that are intended to benefit from it. Some have to lose so others can gain."

"But is it not wrong for the Jaramillos, because they are of a ruthless nature, to destroy a way of life to gain their own advantage?"

"Put that way, I expect it is, but maybe that's not exactly right—all depending on whose ox is getting gored. . . . Our war had something of the same effect. The South lost, and it was part of the country where there were big plantations worked by slaves—like your peons—and the owners lived a fine, easy life, the same as you and your family. The South lost the war and all that came to an end."

"But was that not a true war? Were not battles fought for the possession of cities?"

"Quite a few—"

"There we have difference," Bravo said flatly. "Jaramillo and those like him, while claiming to represent our government, do not. They represent only themselves and the greedy men who support them.

"There were no great battles in which he was involved; instead, as a thief in the night, he came into such peaceful places as our village. Old people of aristocracy were lined up as criminals and shot dead. Our women were taken off by the soldiers, our men were forced to become followers of such as El Escorpion or suffer death. Our haciendas, the work of a lifetime—of several life-times—were destroyed by fire and cannon. . . . Is that not a difference?"

"Maybe, but we had men like Jaramillo, too—the Quantrells and such—who took advantage of the situation for their own benefit. But war, no matter what kind, is always hell and there's no guarantee that the right side is going to win every time, but after it's all over it seems somehow to have worked out for the best."

Dominguez considered that in silence as they loped on at an easy pace. A short string of wagons approached, the voices of several women within them singing a hymn as they drew abreast and passed.

"It is then you feel that such change—a revolution, it was termed—was good and should be accepted?"

"Not smart enough to answer that, but it's a thing that happens and I reckon will keep on happening to people, and what comes out of it seems to be an improvement."

"It is your belief then that what Jaramillo did to

the old families of the Joaquin Valley and to others who lived there was a good thing?"

"Maybe not good the way you mean it, but I think the people will be better off, eventually, because of what happened. You're proof of that—you and what you intend to do toward giving them—the peons—a new life. The bad part of it is that so much suffering has gone into bringing it about."

"*Aiee*," Dominguez groaned heavily. "So many have died—so many."

"Life's a lot like nature—plenty ruthless when it comes to getting something done. That's not something I thought up but what I've heard my pa say many times."

"There is wisdom in the words," Bravo agreed, "but also it is hard to understand why good men like Carlos and Felipe and Francisco Gomez must die to attain such."

Starbuck, grown weary of the discussion, shook his head, pointed to a yellowish cloud hanging on the horizon.

"That'll be Dodge City."

The vaquero studied the smudge, smiled. "We are near."

"Be there in an hour or so," Shawn said, glancing at the sun. It was directly overhead, a dull, pearl disk hidden behind a thickly overcast sky that had so far failed to produce any rain.

Another wagonload of family and furniture lum-

bered by, the black-whiskered man and his bon-
neted woman raising a hand in greeting as they
passed. Both appeared worn and listless. Like as
not they had been on the move for months, had
many more yet ahead of them.

"There's a big grove of trees just before we get
to town," Starbuck said. "Be a good place for you
to wait while I talk to Earp. You've got my word
I'll come back for you soon as I learn where we
can find Amigo."

The vaquero frowned. "It was not necessary for
you to assure me of that."

"Just wanted to lay it out clear," Shawn replied.

An hour later they reached the thick stand of tall,
spreading trees. Wagons were parked here and
there as weary pilgrims took advantage of the
opportunity to halt, lay over, rest themselves and
their animals before pushing on.

"We'll ride to the far side," Starbuck said. "Near
as I recall there's a stream where—"

Abruptly he pulled up. An arm's length to his
right, Bravo, a quick oath exploding from his lips,
also jerked his horse to a halt as a slim figure
stepped out from behind the trunk of large
sycamore. . . . Sandoval.

The Mexican agent, pistol in his hand, greeted
them with a twisted smile. "We meet again,
senors."

Starbuck stared at the man. Bravo Dominguez
was a taut, silent shape, his dark features set.

"You think to have escaped from me? No one has ever done so, and for this time I have given thanks to the railroad."

The railroad! Shawn swore. He hadn't given any thought to the possibility that Sandoval, left far behind, would climb aboard the train at Las Vegas and quickly make the journey to Dodge. Likely he had been there for days, and knowing that it was their destination, had stationed himself at the edge of town to await them. He shook his head at the man.

"No need for that gun. We'll go to the marshal—"

"You are my prisoners. I have no time for your marshal. We shall return at once to Mexico where you will die—"

"No—you die!" Bravo shouted, and whipped up his weapon.

The gunshots sounded in quick succession, with Sandoval's coming a fraction sooner. The vaquero jolted, rocked sideways on his saddle. Starbuck, reacting instinctively, drew his pistol, fired as the Mexican agent pivoted, brought his weapon to bear on him.

Reflex triggered Sandoval's pistol as he was stumbling backward and going down. The bullet whipped at Starbuck's sleeve, tore a ragged line in the fabric.

Grim, aware of the startled faces turned toward him by nearby campers, Shawn swung off the sorrel. In two long strides he reached the side of

Dominguez. The vaquero sprawled face up on the hard ground, sightless eyes locked to the gray sky above. That he was dead was evident, but Starbuck nevertheless felt for the heartbeat that was not there.

A heaviness settled through him as he studied the stilled, lean features of the man. He was the last of the Scorpion's killers, and now he, too, was dead—the last except for Amigo, who just could be Ben.

24

Starbuck stood motionless in the sullen light, thin clouds of smoke drifting lazily about him. People, attracted by the gunshots, were hurrying up from elsewhere in the grove, and a man and woman at the edge of the road had paused, were looking down in shocked silence at the lifeless bodies sprawled on the hard-baked ground.

"My God!" the man said in a strained voice.

Abruptly Starbuck bent over, and almost angrily, picked up the vaquero's slim figure and laid it across the saddle of his horse, securing it. Farther over he saw the mount Sandoval had no doubt rented from a local livery stable, and ignoring the gaping crowd, led it to the agent's side. The animal was a bit skittish as he lifted Sandoval's body to hang it over the saddle, and the man who had spoken hurried up to assist. When the chore was finished, Shawn turned to him.

"Obliged to you—"

"No thanks necessary. Was a lucky thing you shot first. Man must've been some kind of lunatic."

"You see it happen?"

"Yes, sir, sure did. Me and my wife, both. That one there," he said, pointing at Sandoval, "just up and started firing. Had his gun out, was just waiting for you and your friend."

Starbuck nodded. "Be obliged if you'd ride in with me to see the marshal. I'll be needing a witness."

"Bet your life," the man said, and wheeling, hurried off toward a horse and buggy drawn up under a tree.

Grim, stunned by the quick turn of events, and with the heavy sense of loss still depressing him, Shawn mounted the sorrel. Taking up the reins of Bravo's black and of the bay Sandoval had ridden, he started for town. The man with the buggy, halting long enough to pick up his wife, swung onto the road behind him.

Starbuck rode directly to the jail, and pulling up at the hitchrack, dismounted. Bystanders along the street gathered quickly to gaze at the bodies draped across their saddles, and before he could enter the slant-roofed building with his witnesses, a lawman came out onto the walk.

"What's this?" he demanded sourly.

It wasn't Earp. Shawn looked beyond him in hopes of seeing the marshal with whom he was acquainted inside. The office was empty.

"Name's Starbuck," he said. "Wyatt Earp around anywhere?"

The lawman shook his head as he considered the two bodies, frowning. "He ain't here no more. I'm Jim Masterson, deputy marshal. What're you—a bounty hunter?"

Starbuck said, "No," and gave the details of the shooting, finishing up with an introduction to his witnesses. "Other folks back in the grove saw it, too, I expect, if you want to look into it further."

Masterson questioned the man and his wife briefly, shrugged. "Good enough for me, Starbuck. Be no charges against you long as you keep that gun out of sight while you're in town. . . . You know what brought it about?"

"Some trouble that started in Mexico. I'd like to arrange for the burying—both of them."

Masterson nodded. "Town'll take care of it. I need to notify anybody—kin maybe?"

"The vaquero didn't have any. Other man I can't answer for," Shawn said, and turning thanked the couple for their help as they moved off toward their buggy.

He stood for a brief time watching them climb into the vehicle, a stillness blanking his features, and then as the pair wheeled away, he came back around to Masterson.

"Looking for a man called Amigo," he said in a hesitant voice. "Was coming here to open a saloon, or maybe buy one."

The lawman motioned to the crowd. "Couple of you take these bodies over to Caseman's place. Tell him I'll be along shortly." He swung his attention again to Starbuck, eyes narrowed slightly. "Amigo? What about him?"

A tenseness filled Shawn. "Want to talk to him."

"Why?"

Starbuck rode out a moment or two while he debated the wisdom of a complete answer. Then, "Personal matter."

Masterson flicked a glance at the two men leading off the horses, pivoted, and headed back into his office.

"Reckon you're too late," he said. "Amigo's dead and buried."

Shawn stiffened. If Amigo and Ben were the same man. . . . Wheeling, he hurried after the lawman.

"When?"

Masterson did not reply, continued on until he reached his desk and had sat down in the chair behind it. Taking out a book of some sort from a drawer, he entered the names Shawn had given him of the dead men, made notations beside each. Only then did he look up.

"Amigo—when? Oh, been a month, more or less. Blew in here dripping with cash. Got into a big card game one night at the Alamo. We found him next morning in an alley, dead. Knife wound in the back—and no cash."

Starbuck leaned forward, hands gripping the edge of the desk, face taut. "He have another name besides Amigo?"

Masterson shrugged, reopened the ledger. "Yeah, reckon he did," he replied, and began to thumb through the pages. "Here it is."

The tension within Starbuck heightened. The lawman tipped the book slightly in order to read the writing in the day's poor light. Outside a soft rain had begun to fall, pattering on the roof, lifting small, tan geysers as the drops hammered into the loose dust.

"Real name was Henry Platt. Was from Nebraska. Omaha. Relatives claimed the body."

Shawn drew back slowly, relief coursing through him, mingling with the regret he felt for the deaths of Bravo and his partners. The people of Mexico's Joaquin Valley would never know of the help the men who killed the Scorpion had planned to bring them—not even that their lives had been wasted, in vain.

"You got some claim on Platt?" the lawman asked, closing the book.

"No, thought maybe I knew him. Man I'm looking for is named Friend. Was a chance they were one and the same."

Masterson rubbed his palms together thoughtfully. "Friend? Don't recollect anybody around here by the name."

Shawn smiled. His luck never changed. "Didn't

much expect you had. . . . You say Wyatt Earp's not here anymore?"

"Yeah, pulled up stakes, him and his brothers, and lit out for Arizona Territory. Big silver strike there. Town called Tombstone."

"Tombstone?"

"What they named it, all right, and just about every fiddlefoot west of the Missouri's headed that way, all looking to get rich. Ain't you heard about it?"

Starbuck moved toward the door. "Been tied up and a mite busy—but I'm cut loose now."

"That mean you aim to follow the crowd?"

Shawn glanced back, smiled. "Guess I might as well. If that's where everybody's going there's a chance I'll find who I'm looking for. . . . *Adios*, Marshal—and much obliged."

"Reckon you're welcome," Masterson replied, and watched Starbuck cross to the big sorrel he was riding, brush at the raindrops gathered on the saddle, mount and pull away.

Center Point Publishing

600 Brooks Road ● PO Box 1
Thorndike ME 04986-0001 USA

(207) 568-3717

US & Canada:
1 800 929-9108
www.centerpointlargeprint.com